So he'd come here to sort out his life

Wasn't he doing the very thing she'd set out to do—break away from established patterns? "I know how you feel," Evelyn observed.

"I doubt it," Dane remarked drily.

"Stop it," she said crossly. "You said you know my type, but it doesn't mean you know me. My reasons for coming here are every bit as valid as yours."

Dane's eyebrows climbed in disbelief. "I said I know your type, and I do. My ex-wife, Janice, was made in the same mold."

Anger suffused her. "I wasn't made in any mold," she flung at him. "You're wrong about me. You'll see how well I do here, with or without your help. I'm glad you're staying—you'll be able to eat your words at the end of the month."

VALERIE PARV had a busy and successful career as a journalist and advertising copywriter before she began writing for Harlequin in 1982. She is an enthusiastic member of several Australian writers' organizations. Her many interests include her husband, her cat and the Australian environment. Her love of the land is a distinguishing feature in many of her books for Harlequin. She has recently written a colorful study in a nonfiction book titled *The Changing Face of Australia*. Her home is in New South Wales.

Books by Valerie Parv

HARLEQUIN PRESENTS
1229—MAN WITHOUT A PAST

VALERIE PARV

tasmanian devil

Harlequin Books

TORONTO • NEW YORK • LONDON
AMSTERDAM • PARIS • SYDNEY • HAMBURG
STOCKHOLM • ATHENS • TOKYO • MILAN

Harlequin Presents first edition April 1990
ISBN 0-373-11260-2

Original hardcover edition published in 1989
by Mills & Boon Limited

CHAPTER ONE

AS THE green-clad mound of Frere Island appeared as a speck on the horizon, Evelyn Consett suppressed a shiver. It looked primitive and cold.

'Is it true that Frere is the last land before the Antarctic?' she asked the skipper, Ned Freils.

He nodded. 'There's nothing but ocean until you get to Macquarie Island. Are you sure I shouldn't take you to Bruny? It's much more civilised.'

'I don't own Bruny Island,' she snapped back, then realised how arrogant she sounded. Arrogance wouldn't get her far out here. If things got really tough, she might depend on Ned to come to her aid.

He didn't seem bothered by her attitude. 'I didn't know that anyone owned Frere Island,' he observed.

'It was left to me by my mother,' she explained. 'It's the one piece of property which is traditionally passed down the female line.' To herself, she added that it was just her luck to inherit a rocky little island in the Tasman Sea while the family's vast holdings elsewhere in Tasmania would go to her older brother, Alex.

'It must be nice to own an island,' Ned speculated.

She shrugged. 'I never thought about it. It was just there.'

'Have you been here before?'

The cruiser aquaplaned over a wave and she grabbed a handrail. 'My mother brought me here when I was a child. She used to come here to paint. I'm not the outdoor type, I'm afraid. At least, I wasn't,' she added when Ned shot her a curious look. He was probably wondering why a spoiled heiress whose photo regularly graced the social pages should take herself and a substantial supply of provisions to a rugged offshore island, obviously for an extended stay. She was tempted to explain, just to see his reaction. Then she remembered that the papers would love to get hold of the story, and held her tongue. The fewer people who knew the real reason for this expedition, the less humiliating it would be if she failed.

She brought her head up, oblivious of the seaspray misting her face. She was a Consett. Failure wasn't in her lexicon. She would see out her father's prescribed month on this island if it killed her.

A bitter smile twisted her full lips. Maybe Charlton Consett was hoping the experience would finish her off. He had never hidden the fact that sons were what counted with him. Alex had always been the apple of his eye, and he was now being groomed to succeed their father as head of Consett Consolitated Industries, usually referred to as CCI. Even in these liberated times, there was no place for a woman in CCI's boardroom, no matter how capable.

Well, a month of living by herself on Frere Island should convince her father that his thinking was out of date. She could be an asset to CCI, if only he would give her the chance.

'I don't doubt it,' her father had said in that maddeningly reasonable way of his, when she raised the question. 'As my hostess, you're already an asset to the company.'

'I don't want to spend my life being decorative,' she had insisted, but his smile only became more indulgent.

'You are decorative. You grow more like your dear mother with every passing year.'

Her gaze went automatically to the portrait of Lorna Consett which graced the overmantel. Was she like her mother? It was a compliment if so, for Lorna had been considered a beauty in her short life. Even frozen in oils, her hazel eyes shimmered with life, looming huge in a heart-shaped face. The portrait ended at her swanlike neck, but photos showed how lithe her figure had been, a legacy of her passion for dancing and cross-country skiing. 'Am I really like her?' Evelyn asked her father.

'So much that it pains me sometimes. So you can't be anything but beautiful.'

'It doesn't mean I can't have brains as well,' Evelyn said, emerging from her reverie. 'Mother was clever. Her paintings prove it.'

Her father waved a dismissive hand. 'Being artistic doesn't fit one for the harsh realities of the business world. Lorna understood that.'

The unspoken corollary was, why can't you? Evelyn ignored it. 'This is a new generation,' she said impatiently. 'Why did you bother educating me if you didn't want me to work?'

'In the first place, you badgered me unmercifully to send you to university, and in the second, I need you more at home than as a dime-a-dozen filing-clerk.'

Her mouth dropped open. 'Is that all you think I'm good for?'

He sighed. 'Not necessarily, but even as my daughter, you would still be expected to start at the bottom. Alex did.'

'Alex spent exactly three months at the bottom, as you call it,' she retorted, 'before you made him manager of the export division.'

'Alex showed unusual aptitude for the work,' he explained. The undercurrent of steel in his voice warned her that he was keeping his temper with difficulty.

But she had also inherited the Consett temper. 'Are you saying you don't think I have the same aptitude?' she asked with dangerous calmness.

'How do I know?' he snapped back. 'You've never done anything to prove yourself one way or the other.'

It was the last straw. 'I can't prove myself because you won't give me the chance, yet I won't get the chance until I prove myself. How do I get off this merry-go-round?'

'There are other companies besides CCI,' he suggested. 'You could get a job with one of them.'

'You know why I can't.' She had already tried working for a friend's estate agency until rumours began flying that it was to be taken over by CCI and the agency found itself at the centre of a corporate tug-of-war. The friend had reluctantly asked

Evelyn to leave before the rush of prosperity sent her broke.

'I know, I'm sorry I brought it up,' her father said, remembering the incident. 'It's a hazard of having a famous name, I'm afraid. There is one thing you could do, however.'

'What?' she asked suspiciously.

'You want to prove how independent and resourceful you are. Why not spend some time on your mother's island and see how you get along? You won't start any rumours there.'

Evelyn winced. The island had become hers on her mother's death in a sailing accident ten years ago, but Charlton still called it 'your mother's island'. 'What's the catch?' she asked.

'There's no catch. If you can live for a month on Frere Island, taking care of yourself, I'll think about making a place for you in CCI.'

She shook her head, spinning candyfloss hair around her head. 'Not good enough. I need your firm promise.'

His eyes widened. 'You would seriously consider the proposition?'

The corners of her mouth tilted upwards. 'Did you expect me to throw up my hands in horror? Frere Island has a perfectly good cabin, running water and electricity. As long as you let me take some supplies and don't expect me to forage for my food, staying for a month should be a breeze.'

'Is this the same woman who burns boiling water? And yells the house down if her bathwater is below forty degrees centigrade?'

Colour crept into her cheeks, warming them. 'I'm not as bad as all that.'

'Maybe not, but you have led a sheltered existence. You've never been without servants, even at the farm.'

The farm he referred to was a large dairy property in the Derwent Valley where the family spent many of their holidays. Even there, conditions could hardly be called primitive. 'I milked cows and picked apples there,' she reminded him.

His brows drew together. 'When it suited you. It wasn't as if you spent twelve hours a day picking fruit, or rounding up animals.'

'All the same, I shan't chicken out of the month on Frere Island,' she said, bringing her chin up in a gesture which was more characteristic of her father than either of them realised. 'Do we have a deal or not?'

'You are like your mother,' he conceded. 'Especially when it comes to stubbornness. Very well, we have a deal.'

They solemnly shook hands to seal the bargain. Straight away, she had started to plan her month on the island. Her last task had been to hire Ned Freils to take her and her provisions out to the island by cruiser.

'How often do you call in with supplies?' she asked him now.

'It depends.'

'On what?'

'On whether anyone's staying on Frere. I call out to Bruny regularly and I also take fishing parties out in the Channel, but there's no regular schedule.

It's one of the things I like about this life, being my own boss.'

She had forgotten that there was another cabin on the island. The terms of her inheritance didn't allow her to sell or give the island away, but she was allowed to rent out the cottages. She was happy to let the family solicitor take care of the details. When she checked with him to make sure the main cottage was unoccupied, she hadn't thought to ask whether the other cottage was vacant, too. 'Is anyone staying there now?' she asked Ned.

He ran bony fingers through his hair. 'If there is I'm usually asked to bring supplies, but nobody's asked and I haven't seen any boats around.'

Her breath hissed out in a sigh of relief. She didn't like the idea of sharing the island with some curious holidaymakers. If they knew she owned the island, they would no doubt badger her with complaints and problems. Or worse, they might be celebrity-watchers who would snap her every move with their horrid instant cameras and send the results to the papers.

Ned swung the wheel to avoid some floating debris. 'You sound as if you prefer having the island to yourself. I would have thought you'd rather have some company.'

She would if she could choose her own companions. Under the circumstances, she'd rather be by herself. 'I'm looking forward to the experience,' she said emphatically.

He regarded her keenly from under the greying strands of hair cluttering his eyes. 'You haven't spent much time alone, have you, Miss Consett?'

'Call me Evelyn, please,' she said. 'No, I haven't, which is why I decided to give it a try.'

'Always seeking novelty, aren't you?' he muttered under his breath. She had a feeling he meant her kind, rather than her specifically. He was right. When you had all the money you needed and every other material possession it could buy, you soon became tired of comfort and privilege.

'I suppose it will be an adventure,' she admitted.

'Adventures can backfire, you know.'

'I know, but it isn't as if I'm going to the Antarctic or something. I won't be in any danger.' Her eyes twinkled as she looked at him. 'Just in case Dad asked you to keep an eye on me from a discreet distance.'

Ned looked uncomfortable as he concentrated on steering the cruiser. 'He did ask me to make sure you had everything you needed. But he didn't tell me to look out for you or anything like that.'

Her smile became smug. Maybe Charlton hadn't told Ned to look after her in so many words, but that was his intent. Otherwise he wouldn't have been so ready to let her go to the island alone. Kidnapping was a real possibility these days, and Charlton was properly cautious. He would have made some provisions for her safety, she felt sure.

A shadow passed across her eyes. She realised she had been counting on her father to rescue her if things became too uncomfortable. What if he hadn't made any such provisions and she was really on her own?

At last they passed the twin peaks of Bruny Island and the boat began to wallow in the open sea.

Behind them Cape Bruny lighthouse grew steadily smaller, and they passed the cluster of small islands known as the Friars. Ahead of them, the larger mass of Frere loomed like an abbot over a flock of grey-cowled monks.

As a child, she had learned that Frere was originally a mountain-top which became an island in prehistory, when the sea flooded the lower slopes and cut the peak off from the main island of Tasmania.

Studying the landforms, she began to feel the thrill of ownership. The peanut-shaped island had twin peaks to the north and a small hat-shaped peak now visible to the east. All of it was hers. It was the only thing in the world which she truly owned independently of her father's holdings.

Eagerly she took in the forest and fern-clad hills, fringed by rocky outcrops falling away to the sea. She remembered that there was fresh water available and looked forward to discovering the streams and dells at the centre of the island. Unconsciously her slender body craned forwards, as if urging the cruiser on.

Watching her, Ned smiled indulgently. She might think this was a great adventure, but she was in for a shock when reality caught up with her. Here, there were no servants or cooks, just the barest amenities—and a few surprises as well.

He schooled his features into a mask of composure. He shouldn't laugh. This was going to be harder than she imagined, and he hoped she wouldn't find it too daunting. For all her privileges, she was basically a nice kid—a lot like his own daughter, he realised. Except that, at twenty-four, Judy was now married with a baby. Their lives were hardly comparable.

With the skill of long practice, he steered the thirty-footer into the shallows of a small bay which ended in a rough timber jetty. They were soon tied up there and he began off-loading the supplies. 'Would you like a hand to get these up to the cottage?'

She shook her head. She didn't want Ned telling her father that she couldn't even carry her own supplies. In fact, her heart sank at the sight of so many boxes to be carried to the cottage, but she kept her voice light. 'I can manage. I've got plenty of time.'

'Very well. I'll tell your Dad you got here safely, and I'll call back in a fortnight to see if you need anything.'

Her courage faltered. 'Two weeks? How do I get in touch with you if I need you before then?'

'There's a phone in the cabin, but I'm out in the boat during the day so the best time to call is at night. I'll come up and give you a quick tour, then I must be off.'

'Thanks. You're very kind.' She was glad that he wasn't leaving her alone just yet, and let him lead the way to the cabin. From her childhood visits, she remembered that it was up ahead, hidden in the trees, a few hundred yards away from the jetty.

Her heart sank when she saw it. Built of hand-sawn logs, the house dated from the convict era in the eighteen-nineties. The wooden shingle roof was original, and there was a rainwater tank perched on stilts behind the house. She had forgotten how old the cabin was.

Inside, she regarded the one big living-room with apprehension. 'It isn't very modern, is it?'

Ned tried to look reassuring. 'It's sturdier than it appears, or it wouldn't have stood for nearly a century. There's plenty of logs for the fire and we've had good rain so the tank should be full. You'll be all right.'

Ned wrote his number down on a slip of paper and left it near the telephone in the kitchen. Then he explained the workings of the bath heater which was fuelled by wood chips. All too soon, he stood up. 'I wish I could stay longer and help you get settled, but my daughter is expecting me in Kettering for dinner.'

She fixed a brave smile on her face. 'I understand. I'll be fine now.'

'Of course you will.' Even to his own ears, Ned's assurance sounded forced. He was tempted to put her back on the cruiser and take her back with him to the mainland, but Charlton Consett's instructions had been clear. He headed for the door and turned back to salute her. 'See you in a couple of weeks.'

'Goodbye, Ned, and thanks.' The door closed behind him and she sank on to a bentwood rocking-chair which creaked alarmingly. Dust rose in a cloud around her and she sneezed. This was it. For the first time in her life, she was totally dependent on her own resources.

'You asked for it,' she told herself. 'This is your passport to a new life.' Provided it didn't kill her first, she added to herself.

She was postponing the task of moving her supplies from the jetty to the cottage, she knew, but she decided to take a walk around the island while the sun was still warm and the sky invitingly blue. 'Just to get my bearings,' she told herself.

The island was small enough to walk around in two hours, so she couldn't get lost. She set off down a narrow path which she was sure she remembered from visits with her mother.

On this spring day, the air was heavy with the scent of wild flowers. The blossoms attracted birds of every variety, from the native black currawongs to noisy yellow wattlebirds.

If her memory was reliable, she would soon come to Monk's Pool, where a miniature waterfall plunged into a gorge, creating a picturesque fresh-water lagoon. Around her, ancient Huon pines and giant Man ferns filtered the sunlight, creating mosaic patterns on the forest floor. She had a sense of stepping back in time, to some primeval part of Tasmania's past.

She heard the waterfall before she saw it. The path ended in a rocky outcrop and the pool sparkled below her, shaded by a thicket of tree ferns cloaking the slope which led down to the water.

The bird calls gave way to another sound. She listened in amazement, then realised that it sounded like someone humming. Then she saw the man, and instinctively drew back into the shelter of the ferns before he saw her.

Feeling apprehensive, she peered through the fern fronds, prepared to find that she had imagined the man. But he was still there, large as life and certainly twice as handsome. He had evidently been swimming in the pool and was towelling himself dry. Even from behind he was an impressive figure, with wide, well-muscled shoulders which tapered to a narrow waist and lean hips. His legs were long and braced apart as he dried himself. When he lifted the towel to his ash-coloured hair, she saw that he was naked. The mahogany hue of his skin was unmarred by patches of white, so he must often swim like this.

He must be a day-visitor to the island, she decided. She was tempted to leave quietly before he discovered her presence. But her gaze was drawn back to him. She found herself willing him to turn around so that she could see his face, then her colour heightened as she realised she would see much more than that if he turned.

She chided herself for behaving foolishly, watching him from afar. She owned the island. She should announce herself and order him off her property. The fact that he looked like a Greek god arising out of the water had nothing to do with anything.

About to act on the thought, she parted the ferns and moved forward, but her foot caught in a tree-root and she slithered helplessly down the slope to land at the man's feet.

His startled gaze raked her. 'Who the devil are you?'

Scrambling to her feet, she brushed dirt and leaves from her clothes, thankful that her pride was the only thing she had injured. 'I was about to ask you the same thing,' she said.

His hands tightened on the towel as if he was wishing it was her neck. 'You first. I wasn't the one hiding in the bushes like some peeping Thomasina.'

'I wasn't hiding,' she began, then stopped. 'All right, I was, but only because I was surprised to find someone else on the island.'

His pale blue Peter O'Toole eyes swept over her. 'As you can see, I wasn't expecting company either, so I suppose that makes us even.'

She could see a great deal, she realised, now that she was standing in front of him. It was an effort to keep her eyes from straying below the level of his chest. 'I'm sorry for spying on you,' she said, hearing her voice come out low and husky. 'I suppose you came here for a day's privacy.'

His eyebrows, which were a deeper ash colour than his hair, lifted quizzically. 'More like a few months, in fact.'

'A few months? You can't be staying here?'

'Why not? People rent these cottages all the time.'

It was time to make a few things clear. 'I know that. You see I'm Evelyn Consett. I own this island.'

He seemed unimpressed. 'So?'

'So you can't go on staying here.'

His blue-eyed gaze hardened slightly. 'Your solicitor thought differently when he drew up a perfectly valid six-month lease for me.'

As her father's daughter, she was well aware of the implications of a lease. She chewed her lower lip while her thoughts raced. 'I didn't know. I leave these matters to my solicitor, and I didn't think to ask him if both cabins were vacant. Ned Freils, the boatman, assured me no one had ordered supplies to be delivered here.'

'I have my own boat and take care of myself.'

Yes, she thought, he would be the sort who could take care of himself. She was furious with herself for not checking on the other cottage right at the start. She had a feeling that getting this tenant to leave might be difficult. Yet she couldn't spend a month here alone with a strange man, however prepossessing he looked. He could be Jack the Ripper for all she knew.

Already she could be in danger, and she couldn't even contact Ned until nightfall. Then common sense returned. Her solicitor wouldn't have let the cottage without obtaining references. She breathed a little easier. 'Might I know your name?' she asked as disarmingly as she could.

His wide shoulders lifted in a careless shrug. 'Dane Balkan, if it means anything to you.'

'Should it?'

'Probably not. I'm just one of the world's working stiffs, trying to get away from civilisation for a while to recharge my batteries.'

'And I've spoiled it for you.' Her tone was deliberately soothing. Then she delivered the *coup de grâce*. 'I'll gladly pay you for cutting your holiday short.'

His smile was sweet reason itself. 'There's no need for that, Miss Consett.'

'Call me Evelyn, please. Then you'll agree to leave the island without payment?'

'No payment is needed, because I don't plan on leaving.'

She had never felt so helpless. 'But you have to. We can't stay here together.'

'I don't see any problem. You can keep to your end of the island and I'll keep to mine.'

It was a reasonable compromise, but she wasn't used to compromising. She couldn't even explain to herself why his leaving was so important. There was something so overwhelmingly masculine about him that she felt threatened by his presence. He made her feel vulnerable and it bothered her. 'Whoever you are, Mr Dane Balkan, you're no gentleman,' she flung at him. 'Or you would see why we can't possibly share the island.'

'I never claimed to be a gentleman,' he assured her equably. 'There is another solution, though.'

She clutched at the straw. 'What is it?'

'You could go back to where you came from. You're like a fish out of water in a place like this. I'll bet you've never slept without air-conditioning in your life.'

Aware that it was true, she looked away. Then she was assailed by a vision of her father's face if she came home now, without having spent even one night on the island. 'I can't leave,' she said unhappily.

'Why not? They ended transportation to these islands with the end of the convict era.'

It was a great temptation to stamp her foot. 'Will you be serious? I'm not here for any crime, unless you count wanting to prove myself as a crime.'

She had his interest at last. 'Is that what you're doing here?'

She felt a surge of optimism. Maybe the truth would convince him of the importance of her stay here, and persuade him to leave without a fuss. 'Yes. My father bet me I couldn't stay here for a month, looking after myself. I intend to prove that I can.'

Some of the cynicism returned to his face. 'What's the prize—a new designer wardrobe from Paris?'

His comment stung, but she masked her response. 'No, a job with his organisation.'

'Do you really want to work for a living?'

'Is it so unusual? Lots of people do.'

'And just as many people don't.' She had a feeling he was referring to someone in particular, but their acquaintance was too new for her to ask, although her curiosity was piqued. 'Most women would give their eye-teeth for your life-style,' he added.

It was getting harder to remain reasonable. 'They might not be so eager if they tried it for a while,' she snapped back.

He gave her a look of grudging respect. 'You're really committed to staying here, aren't you?'

Her chin came up. 'Yes, I am.'

'Unfortunately, so am I. The island happens to suit me for the present. But we shouldn't have much to worry about. It should all work itself out.'

Her eyes narrowed in suspicion. He sounded like her father when things went the way he wanted them to. 'What makes you so sure?'

'I know your type. You won't last a week living here, far less a month. So the problem will soon solve itself.'

As she stared at him, too stunned to retaliate, he slung the towel around his hips, knotted it with an aggressive gesture, and strode off. He looked like some latter-day Tarzan with a monogrammed towel for a loincloth, she thought as she watched him go.

He was nearly out of sight before she regained her power of speech. 'We'll see about that,' she yelled at his unrelenting back. 'We'll see about that, Mr Dane Balkan.'

CHAPTER TWO

ALTHOUGH the day was mild, Evelyn's throat was arid by the time she retraced her steps to her cottage. She blamed her agitated mood on her encounter with Dane Balkan. He had a nerve, expecting her to leave her own island to him.

A vision of him with crystal droplets of water beading his magnificent body rose before her, and her heart began to pound from more than her brief exertions. In their short acquaintance, she had been more aware of him than of any other man she had met. She screwed up her eyes in concentration. It wasn't just his Iron Man looks, although they stayed in her mind. Perhaps it was his air of absolute assurance, as if he and not she owned the island. He had called himself a working stiff, but it was hard to believe about such a man.

Her head came up and her eyes flew open. Why was she letting him make such an impact on her? She would be better employed trying to think of a way around the problem of his lease.

Deciding that a cup of coffee would help her to think, she rested a hand on the cabin door, then remembered that her supplies were waiting on the jetty. Until she brought them up there would be no coffee. She was sorry now that she had refused Ned's offer of help.

She was even sorrier when she saw the mess awaiting her. When she left them, the cardboard cartons holding her groceries had been neatly stacked. Now they were scattered all over the jetty, some torn open so their contents spilled on to the silver timbers. Pieces of fruit bobbed in the shallows like flotsam from a shipwreck, and a carpet of rice and pasta crunched underfoot.

The chaos was so bewildering that she stood and stared at it in amazement, unable to explain what had happened. Then understanding dawned. 'That bastard!' she seethed, and turned on her heel.

She remembered that the other cottage was a few hundred yards beyond the waterfall, in a clearing of its own, surrounded by tall trees.

Dane was there, all right. The clear ringing sound of his axe as he chopped wood reached her ears as she strode, grim-faced, along the narrow track.

Her plan to burst from the clearing and confront him died as soon as she saw him. He was an awesome sight and she caught her breath, almost forgetting why she was here. He stood in the centre of a circle which was layered with chips and bark. His powerful legs were wide apart and his arms were upraised, both hands gripping the axe as it flew through the air. Down it came in a blur of movement, biting a wedge out of the hardwood log and sending chips flying everywhere.

Mesmerised, she watched him repeat the movement again and again until perspiration glistened on his bare chest and shoulders. His jeans rode low on his hips, emphasising his lean proportions. He wore no gloves, and gripped the axe handle as delicately as if it were a surgeon's scalpel. The incisions in the timber were surgically precise, she noticed, as the cut deepened.

The air was fragrant with the sweet smell of timber, mixed with the odours of earth and decaying leaves. The widening cut reminded her of a ripe water-melon with a slice removed.

With a splintering sound, the log split into two neat halves the right size for the firebox of their wood stoves. He tossed the pieces on to an already substantial pile and straightened, hefting the axe as he eased his back muscles.

His sharp gaze penetrated the curtain of leaves and recognition was immediate. 'Spying on me again?' he demanded.

Feeling foolish for being caught a second time, she emerged into the full glare of his inspection. There was no point in denying it. She had been spying, but only because the sight of him using his magnificent body to the full was so startling. She recovered her voice and her anger with it. 'I came to tell you that it won't work.'

Irritation clouded his expression. 'I'm not in the mood to play games. What won't work?'

'Your petty attempt at sabotage,' she responded. 'I know you don't want me here, but there was no need to damage my supplies.'

His puzzlement seemed to be genuine. 'Damage your supplies? I don't know what you're talking about.'

'I left my stuff on the jetty, and when I went to get it, it looked as if wild animals had trampled through everything.'

'And you think it was my doing?'

'We are the only people on the island,' she reminded him coldly.

His gaze was equally glacial as he swung the axe down and leant on the handle. 'Maybe the only people, but not the only living creatures.'

'Oh, come on, you can't expect me to believe that some little animal opened those cardboard boxes and scattered the contents everywhere?'

Her scorn left him unmoved. 'I'll show you what little animals can do, Miss High and Mighty.'

Before she could protest, he tossed the axe aside and took a firm grip on her arm. She found herself being hustled back along the path towards the jetty. The raw timber fragrance receded and was replaced by the disturbingly male scent of him, heightened by his recent workout. She couldn't help bumping against him as he urged her along. To her touch, his body was every bit as solid as it appeared. Still heated from his exertions, he radiated a warmth which penetrated her clothes. It played havoc with her body temperature.

Distracting though the sensation was, she resisted it and tugged at her hand held firmly in his. 'Stop. I'm not going anywhere with you.'

His pace didn't falter. 'You started this. I'm going to finish it.'

Again it occurred to her that she was totally at his mercy here. 'How?'

'You'll soon see.'

She could have sat down and refused to budge, but pride and curiosity made her determined to keep up with his fast-moving strides along the bush path.

Her free hand brushed at the low-growing bushes which swung across her face. One or two stung her cheeks when she was too slow to react. By the time they emerged on to the shore, she was burning with anger and humiliation. 'You'll regret this,' she vowed in a low voice which vibrated with fury.

His gaze flicked back over his shoulder. 'Why? Because you're a Consett?'

She had been about to remind him who he was manhandling, but his comment showed his disdain for her background.

'What has my family ever done to you?' she asked instead.

They had almost reached the jetty where her provisions lay scattered over the ground. 'Not your family in particular, but your kind, so spoilt that they never stop to consider other people's feelings.'

'How do you know I'm like that? We've only just met,' she said, provoked in spite of herself.

'True. Yet in our short acquaintance you've tried to order me off the island and accused me of something I didn't do. Look here!'

He released her hand and she rubbed the wrist, more for show than because he had inflicted any real damage. Then she looked where he was pointing and saw what shock had prevented her from seeing before. The flour spilling over the ground was pock-marked with dog-sized footprints.

But they weren't dog tracks, she saw as she crouched down and examined them. They made an odd pattern. One print was followed by two, more or less side by side, then one. 'What could have made these tracks?' she asked, glancing up to where

Dane Balkan towered over her, hands on hips, waiting.

'So you admit they aren't my footprints?' he said in a voice which dripped sarcasm.

'Of course they aren't.' She straightened, although his additional height still gave him an advantage. 'All right, I'm sorry I accused you unjustly. I was so shocked to find my provisions in such a mess...' When he showed no signs of unbending, her voice tailed off. 'What do you want me to say?'

Some of the tension ebbed out of him, and he relaxed visibly. 'Your apology is accepted. The supplies were damaged by a Tasmanian Devil.'

She looked at him in frank disbelief. 'A Tasmanian Devil? I thought they only came out at night.'

He nodded. 'They are nocturnal. But there's one on the island which doesn't seem to know the rules.'

Her spirits began an upward spiral. So he wasn't the implacable tyrant he appeared. He had a soft spot for animals. It was a weakness they shared. 'Is it a pet of yours?' she asked.

His lips thinned, but there was a glint of humour in the pale eyes. 'She thinks she is. I didn't try to tame her. She adopted me, so I called her Henrietta. She comes to be fed every evening.'

Evelyn cast a glance at the chaos surrounding them. 'It looks as if she decided not to wait.'

'I'm afraid so. But she won't have eaten much. They're carnivores, unless you had any chickens among this lot.'

She shook her head. 'I took the frozen food up to the cabin with me when I got here. The rest was mostly cans and dry goods.'

'Just as well.'

The silence between them grew while she wondered how to fill it. He solved the problem for both of them. 'What made you think I would do this to you?'

She spread her hands wide apart. 'I don't know. You seemed so annoyed to find me here.'

'But I told you so to your face, didn't I?' he said quietly.

'Yes, you did. I suppose you wouldn't have done if you were planning to get rid of me some other way.'

He took a step forward and cupped her chin in one hand, gently lifting her face so their eyes met. 'Remember this, Evelyn Consett. I'm a man of my word. I get what I want by fair means, or not at all. Is that clear?'

She was drowning in the dusky blue pools of his eyes. His gaze held her in thrall and it was an effort to summon her voice. 'Yes, it's clear. I'm sorry I doubted you at all.'

'Good. I'm glad we understand each other.'

He looked away towards the ocean and the spell was broken. She bent and righted a cardboard box, then piled packets of food into it. He moved away and settled himself on one of the wooden piles supporting the jetty, crossing his arms over his chest. His scrutiny made her feel wooden and awkward. She looked up at him, feeling irritated. 'You could give me a hand, you know.'

A smile tugged at the corners of his mouth. 'I thought you wanted to do it all by yourself.'

Damn him for remembering. Her full lips tightened into a line and she averted her eyes, giving the clean-up all her attention. 'You're quite right,' she ground out. 'I won't ask for your help again.'

This time he gave the smile full rein until it was all she could do not to heave a sack of rice at him. 'I wish I could count on it.'

'Count on it.' She wouldn't ask him for help if she was dying, she resolved as she added more packets to the box. When she had salvaged all she could, she collected up the tins which had rolled all over the place. Some had lost their labels, so she would have to take pot luck with the contents. But if she ended up eating tinned fruit on toast she wouldn't utter a word of complaint. Never would she give Dane Balkan the satisfaction.

'That's the spirit,' he said after he had watched her for a while.

In spite of herself, she was curious. 'What do you mean?'

'You're mad as hell right now, aren't you?'

The laughter in his voice made the hairs on the back of her neck stand out more. The blood was already singing in her veins from all the stooping and standing, and his taunt brought an added flush to her cheeks. 'What do you expect? My thanks that you're helping me to be more self-sufficient?'

'Something of the sort. It was what you came here for, wasn't it?'

'I came to prove to my father that I could stand on my own two feet. Not to amuse some mean-spirited drop-out who sets wild animals on defenceless women.'

He didn't even try to conceal his amusement. 'There you go again, making rash judgements. What makes you think I'm a drop-out?'

'Why else would you be living here, hiding from society? You don't look like the beachcomber type. For all I know, you could be wanted for computer fraud or some such on the mainland.'

Some of the amusement left his face. 'I should be glad you think I'm a white-collar criminal, at least. But the only thing you got right was the part about me hiding from society, and I wasn't aware it was a crime.'

She waited for him to elaborate, but he forestalled her by hefting a carton on to his shoulder. 'We're in for some rain soon. I'll give you a hand to get these to your cabin before it starts.'

While they were talking, ominous charcoal clouds had clustered overhead, she saw now. With alacrity, she grabbed another box and followed Dane. Her curiosity about him was fully aroused, but she would have to satisfy it later. She dared not risk having her remaining provisions spoiled, either by rain or by the mischievous Henrietta.

Even with Dane's help it took several trips before her supplies were stowed safely away. By then large drops of rain were splattering against the shingled roof. She looked at Dane, shamefaced. 'I'm sorry for calling you those names,' she offered.

He regarded her keenly. 'Then you don't think I'm a mean-spirited drop-out who sets wild animals on young women?'

'It was a bit extreme, I admit.'

'Which part? The one about me being mean-spirited or training wild animals to attack defence-less women?'

'All of it,' she had to concede. She doubted whether he could ever be mean-spirited. Just because he hadn't rushed to help her repack the supplies didn't make him ungenerous. Hadn't she insisted she could make it on her own? And she could hardly blame him when an animal acted on its instincts, no doubt attracted by the smell of her food. 'I really am sorry.'

A smile played around the corners of his wide mouth. 'Apology accepted—again,' he said, emphasising the last part.

Her smooth brow creased. 'I've been making a habit of apologising to you since I got here, haven't I?'

'It beats accusing me of dastardly deeds,' he pointed out.

'All right, no more accusations,' she promised. 'How about a cup of coffee instead?'

He pulled a chair out from the scrubbed pine table and folded his considerable height on to it. 'What a good idea. Can you manage the stove?'

'Of course I can,' she said a little too quickly. 'The previous tenant left plenty of firewood.' She indicated the pile of logs stacked in a vast metal box beside the stove. 'All I have to do is light it.'

Suddenly she wished she hadn't been so quick to assure him she could cope. She had never lit a wood stove in her life. This one looked huge and daunting, its grate blackened by years of hard polishing. Tentatively, she lifted a log from the box and looked at the stove. There was a little door in front which must be the firebox. One-handed, she jiggled it open. Sure enough, there was a layer of grey ash in the bottom. She thrust the log inside, then looked around. Where had the matches ended up?

Dane was ahead of her, offering a box of matches before she could ask. She took them silently and turned back to the firebox. Where did one light such a monster?

Half a dozen matches later, the wood still refused to catch. Tears of frustration prickled at the backs of her eyes. If only Dane wasn't watching her every move. 'Still think you can manage?' he asked after a while.

'Oh, all right, you do it,' she said, and tossed the matches on to the table. She should never have come to this horrible place, to be laughed at because she couldn't do something as simple as lighting a stove.

'There is a trick to it, you know,' Dane said behind her. Reluctantly she turned around. She had better pay attention if she was to do it herself next time.

She watched closely as he placed a pile of wood chips on top of the larger log, then he crumpled some packing paper from her cartons on top of that. The paper caught light as soon as he touched a match to it, in turn lighting the chips of timber. 'Start with kindling—the small bits of wood. They will light the rest,' he informed her.

He waited until the larger log started to catch fire, then fiddled with another knob he called a damper. 'This gives you control over the intensity of the fire.'

She felt a wave of nostalgia for the modern kitchen of her family's Georgian mansion at Battery Point. It was equipped with every luxury, from the latest microwave oven to an indoor barbecue. An espresso machine kept coffee at the ready. There was no need to battle a fire-breathing monster merely to boil a kettle of water.

'Are you sorry you came?' Dane probed, taking note of her miserable expression.

She brought her chin up, not wanting to admit how she felt. 'I'll cope,' she said grimly. 'I have a lot to learn, but there's plenty of time.'

'A whole month, I know,' he said resignedly. 'Why is surviving here so important to you?'

It was none of his business and her expression told him so. Then she relented, feeling the need to explain her reasons as much to herself as to him. 'Haven't you ever set out to prove something to yourself?' she asked.

'Like climbing a mountain, you mean?'

'Exactly,' she agreed, feeling her spirits lift. Maybe he understood her feelings, after all.

'No,' he said, dashing her hopes. 'I save my energy for challenges which matter. To me, climbing a mountain is like doing a jigsaw puzzle. There's nothing to show for all that effort.'

'Except a sense of achievement and the knowledge that you've pushed yourself to a limit and surpassed it,' she said a little breathlessly.

He looked unimpressed. 'So staying on this island is the mountain you've set out to conquer.'

Her eyes flashed fire at him. 'This isn't a whim, you know. If I can last a month here, Dad will have to make a place for me in his company. Then I'll be able to earn my keep and be of some value. Can't you understand?'

'Frankly, no,' he told her. 'A sense of value doesn't come from outside, from a job or a position in society. It comes from inside you.'

'You make it sound easy, but then you've never been treated as an expensive decoration, more like a pet than a person.'

His thick brows drew together. 'How would you know?'

Had she jumped to another wrong conclusion about him? He was on retreat here, for whatever reason, so maybe he wasn't as self-assured as he appeared. 'Why are you here?' she asked boldly. 'Woman trouble?'

His lip curled derisively. 'You'd know all about it, I suppose? What are you, eighteen?'

With her flowing lemon-meringue hair and heart-shaped features, she did look younger than her years. 'I'm twenty-four,' she said a little defensively.

'Worlds apart,' he murmured. 'I'm thirty-two.'

Her surprised reaction must have given her away. He seemed so worldly-wise that she had expected him to be older. 'And I still have all my teeth and hair, despite my advanced age,' he added, misreading her response.

The kettle began to sing on the stove, claiming her attention. The instant coffee was on top of one of her boxes. She plucked two stoneware mugs from a rack, polished them, then spooned coffee into them. She felt elated. This, she could do. 'Do you take cream or sugar?' she asked.

Luckily he wanted neither, for she had no idea where they were. Normally she liked cream in her coffee, but decided that this was a good time to learn to take it black. Better for the figure, anyway.

She passed him a steaming mug and watched as he sipped it. 'Well?'

'A bit strong, but you'll learn,' he said.

Sipping her own coffee, she shuddered at the strength of it but masked the reaction. 'Mine's fine,' she lied. 'Now tell me, Dane, what do you do?'

It was a common enough question at the parties she attended by the score. She was unprepared for his answer. 'Me? Nothing.'

'I meant before you came here.'

'I was a commodities broker with the Hobart Stock Exchange.'

She was taken aback. He had looked so at home here that she had expected something different. Brokers were the dull men who made their living buying and selling shares, bonds and futures. From the little she had seen, they all suffered from tunnel vision. They thought nothing of spending eighteen hours a day at the office, then going home to continue wheeling and dealing when the overseas markets opened at five or six o'clock Australian time.

The fact that Dane had left the world of international finance to come here meant he must be aware of the pitfalls. 'So you came here to sort out your life. That's very romantic,' she observed.

He frowned. 'It isn't romantic, it's strictly practical. I didn't like the people I was mixing with, either professionally or socially. So I called a halt.'

Thoughtfully, she sipped her coffee, adjusting to its strength so that she no longer shuddered. Wasn't he doing the very thing she herself had set out to do—break away from established patterns? 'I know how you feel,' she observed.

'I doubt it,' he remarked drily.

'Stop it,' she said crossly. 'You said you know my type, but it doesn't mean you know me. My reasons for coming here are every bit as valid as yours.'

His expressive eyebrows climbed into an arch of disbelief. 'So you think I don't know you. Well, let's see. You went to school at Collegiate, did your HSC, then went on to university to do your degree. You worked part-time in a friend's business but gave it up. Your favourite designers are Jenny Kee and Trent Nathan. You shop at Zampatti and Renata Boutique in Centrepoint, and you meet your girlfriends for "cuisine moderne" at *Dear Friends*. Shall I continue?'

It must be coincidence that he had named some of her favourite people and places. 'You must have read all that in a magazine,' she insisted.

'I didn't have to. I married you.'

Now she was thoroughly confused. 'What?'

'I said I know your type, and I do. My ex-wife Janice was made in the same mould as you were.'

Anger suffused her and she gripped her cup in two hands before the spilling coffee betrayed her feelings. 'I wasn't made in any mould,' she flung at him. 'You may have been disappointed by your wife, but probably because she was your better and you couldn't keep up. It's her I feel sorry for, not you.'

As soon as she saw the colour leave his face, she regretted her outburst. What on earth had possessed her to say such an awful thing, when she didn't even believe it in the first place? As he stood up, she reached for him, but he brushed her hand aside. 'I rest my case. You are all alike, and you stick up for one another. Janice was just the same.'

The apology she had been framing died on her lips. 'You're wrong about me,' she said hotly, not sure why she felt so driven to defend herself. 'You'll see how well I do here, with or without your help. In a way, I'm glad you're staying, so that you'll be around to eat your words at the end of the month.'

Her anger left him unmoved. Instead, she could have sworn there was a gleam in the dusky eyes. 'It looks like this month will be a lesson for both of us.'

Before she could guess his intentions, he had divested her of her coffee-cup and pulled her into his arms. Caught off guard, she sagged against him and was immediately conscious of the virile strength in his hard body. 'What are you doing?' she asked, thinking she ought to struggle. She certainly shouldn't enjoy the feeling of being in his arms.

'Since we're going to be alone here for so long, we might as well get to know one another.'

She twisted her head to one side to avoid his questing mouth, which was within inches of her own. 'I don't want to know you, not like this.'

His lips grazed her burning cheek and a shivery sensation engulfed her. 'Yes, you do. Your body language tells me so.'

Damn his perception! For, despite her efforts to remain unmoved, her inner being was aflame with an excitement which made her feel as if she had only been half-alive until this moment.

His hands travelled across the small of her back, their heat scorching through her shirt as he pressed her against him. It was all she could do not to mould her soft contours against his hard ones. 'Still sure it's wise to stay?' he murmured into her ear.

All trace of arousal vanished as she understood his meaning. This embrace was only another ploy to persuade her that she ought to leave the island. By letting his touch affect her, she was playing right into his hands, in more ways than one.

At once, she stopped resisting and nestled against him. Trying to ignore the answering stirrings in her body, she fought for control and whispered the first thoughts which came to mind, into his ear. 'You're right, this will liven up my stay. And I thought it was going to be dull.'

She wasn't surprised when he ended the embrace abruptly. 'I'd better go before the rain sets in.' His voice was intriguingly low-pitched.

She feigned disappointment. 'You aren't leaving?'

'Only the cottage and only for now,' he confirmed. 'We have the whole month, remember? There's no point in rushing things.'

As long as he remembered it, she thought as he left. He had intended to scare her away with his advances and she had called his bluff. Round one to Evelyn.

She went to the window and watched him stride down the bush path, his broad back hunched against the rising wind. The urge to go after him was almost overwhelming.

Gradually she became aware that her response hadn't been as much of an act as she thought. Suddenly her cabin seemed achingly lonely.

CHAPTER THREE

SHOCK brought Evelyn bolt upright in bed, her dream shattered. It took her several seconds to remember where she was and connect the jangling noise which had disturbed her with the telephone. She grimaced. Unlike her cordless model at home, this telephone was firmly fixed in the kitchen downstairs.

Hoping that her caller wasn't the impatient type, she thrust her feet into lambswool slippers and flung her velvet gown around her shivering shoulders. She was out of breath by the time she brought the receiver to her ear. 'Hello?'

'It's Donna Radcliffe, Miss Consett. I have your father on the line.'

He could have called her himself instead of having his secretary do it, she thought, gripping the phone more tightly. Along with the irritation she recognised disappointment. Unconsciously, she had been hoping that the caller was Dane. The memory of his embrace was still vivid, even though she understood the strategy behind it. He knew she hadn't been fooled, so he might have called to apologise.

Her fantasy was interrupted by her father's gruff voice coming on the line. 'Just wanted to see how you're doing.'

41

'I'm fine, thanks, Dad,' she said, sure this wasn't what he expected to hear.

'Managing to eat all right?'

Her sigh whispered into the telephone. 'I only arrived yesterday. There wasn't time for a banquet before bed.'

Nor much hope of making the stove co-operate, she could have added, but didn't care to give him the satisfaction. She had forgotten to keep the stove stocked with wood, and the wretched appliance had gone out. Without any more kindling she couldn't relight it. As a result, she had dined on sandwiches and washed in cold water before retiring early.

The only pleasant surprise had been the loft bed. With its feather mattress and cosy down quilt, it was blissfully comfortable. Wide enough for three people, it had enfolded her like a lover's arms, and she had slept much better than she had expected to. Tired out by her exertions, she told herself with a wry smile. She had done more walking and carrying yesterday than in a normal week at home.

'I rang to tempt you home for the weekend,' her father said.

'Not missing me already?' she asked. The opposite was more likely to be true. 'Our deal is that I stay here for a full month, remember?'

'I know, but I just found out that your Aunt Alice is flying in for a couple of days before she leaves on her next promotional tour, and I thought . . .'

You thought I'd forget the whole thing and come home, she said to herself. Alice Newcombe, her mother's younger sister, was a successful travel-writer whom Evelyn liked. Unfortunately, she was also a demanding house-guest. Evelyn was usually the only person who could please her. She should have known that her father had another reason for his call besides her welfare. 'Sorry, Dad, a deal's a deal,' she said firmly.

'Don't be ridiculous. I need you here.'

But only to pander to her aunt, she thought bleakly. If she backed down now, he would never respect her right to lead her own life. 'I understand your problem, and I'd like to help, but I want to see this through first,' she insisted, trying to keep a tremor out of her voice. She had never contested his wishes before.

'Damn it, you can have the job. Just come home and bail me out with Alice.'

Her teeth gnawed at her lower lip. Could it really be so easy? There was only one answer. 'Thanks, Dad, but I'd rather earn my position than be given it by grace and favour.'

She could almost hear the wheels working in his mind. 'In that case, my girl, you will earn it. Turn up here one day before the month is up and you lose. No more talk of jobs around me. Is that clear?'

'Yes, Dad.' They were the terms they had agreed to in any case. She hadn't treated this like a game, although apparently that was how her father had seen it. Well, she had burned her bridges behind her now. She took a steadying breath. 'Give my love to Aunt Alice, won't you, Dad?'

But he had already hung up the phone, and static crackled in her ear.

Thoughtfully, she replaced the receiver. She had intended to tell her father about Dane's presence on the island, but he hadn't given her a chance.

Sharp pains shooting through her feet reminded her that she had more immediate concerns. Her feet and hands felt like blocks of ice, but until she had conquered the wood-chip heater in the bathroom there was no chance of a warming bath. She would have to settle for another splash wash. As she went upstairs to dress, she decided that, if this was nearly summer, winter on Frere Island didn't bear thinking about.

What was Dane doing now? The thought rose unbidden, and she paused with her polo-necked sweater half-way over her head. He looked like the hardy type who jogged before breakfast.

Her gaze strayed to the window which was shaded by an ancient eucalypt, its branches alive with birds. Below her window snaked the bush path which led to Dane's cottage. So vivid was her image of him as a jogger that she half expected to see him come pounding along the path, his long, muscular legs pumping like pistons as they ate up the ground. The path was deserted except for a couple of sulphur-crested cockatoos scratching for food.

She smoothed the sweater over her full breasts, and her attention shifted to her silhouette reflected in the dresser mirror. As she reached for her brush and began pulling it through the blonde cascade around her shoulders, she wondered how she compared with Janice Balkan.

The name seemed familiar. They might have worked for the same charities. After a while, the functions became a blur to Evelyn, so they could have met without her remembering it. But, despite Dane's accusation, she wasn't a Janice. Many times she had wished she could send a cheque instead of attending yet another charity ball in person.

With a sweeping gesture, she pulled the sweater off and dropped it on the floor, then reached for one with a less constricting neckline. Thinking about Dane had brought a tightness to her throat, as if she were short of oxygen. It didn't make any sense.

A sound at the window made her jerk around. Her eyes widened in alarm at the sight of a face framed there. It was Dane. She tugged her sweater down over her breasts. 'What do you think you're doing?'

Dane levered the window up. 'I thought you'd be dressed by now. I'm about to fix your roof. You have quite a few loose shingles. I'm surprised they didn't leak during last night's rain.'

They had, but she was damned if she would admit it. His blatant inspection of her long legs which were still innocent of any covering was disconcerting enough. She wasn't giving him the idea she needed him. 'I didn't ask for your help,' she insisted.

'You didn't have to. I'm offering.'

The roguish way his sparkling eyes swept her up and down sent an unexpected wave of heat surging along her limbs. For an insane moment, he sounded as if he was offering much more than to fix her roof. Her tongue darted across suddenly dry lips. 'I'm refusing your offer, thank you all the same.'

Despite her best efforts, her husky tones carried an echo of his double meaning.

He rested his forearms on the sill, his massive shoulders filling the opening. 'You could regret this, you know.'

Her long lashes fluttered against hot cheeks. 'In what way?'

'You could get inundated if there's a real storm. Last night was just a shower by comparison with some of the downpours we get here.'

His businesslike tone broke the spell. Of course they were only talking about the roof. She wondered if her irritation was partly due to disappointment that his offer wasn't more personal. She reminded herself that his motives were the same as her father's: to prove that Evelyn couldn't fix anything more challenging than her hair.

Both of them wanted to see her fail, she thought savagely, her father because he didn't want to lose his social secretary, and Dane so that he could have the island to himself again. They were in for a disappointment. 'I'll take my chance with the rain,' she flung at him. 'I can manage perfectly well without your help.'

His teasing expression fled as his eyes became hooded and unreadable. 'Suit yourself,' he said, and started down his ladder.

Remorse overcame her with a rush. She wasn't usually so ungrateful, and Dane could have genuinely wanted to help. She rushed to the window and leaned out across the sill in time to see him shouldering the ladder. His broad back was turned to her, the muscles rippling with each movement. He hefted the ladder as if it was made of matchwood. 'Dane, wait,' she called, but he gave no sign of having heard her.

Conflicting emotions warred inside her as she finished dressing, then breakfasted on fresh fruit and a glass of Long-Life milk. She already regretted her rudeness to Dane, but still suspected his motives. After her father's call this morning, it was easy to think that Dane also wanted her to fail. Hadn't he already tried to scare her away once?

She had seen through him last night. Was he likely to be more sincere in the cold light of day? There was one way to find out.

He was chopping wood again when she went in search of him. The thunk-thunk of axe against timber made an angry sound, as if he was working off his annoyance with her on the wood pile.

When she joined him in the clearing, he gave no sign of noticing her, although his arm muscles tensed, disturbing the steady rhythm of his chopping.

'I wanted to talk to you about this morning,' she began.

The axe rose and fell steadily. 'Go ahead and talk.'

'Can't you stop that for a minute?'

A streak of silver flew across her path, followed by a whirruping sound as the axe blade embedded itself in a log. Dane wiped his hands along the sides of his jeans, leaving trails of sawdust down his hips. 'You made yourself clear this morning. What more is there to say?'

'You caught me off guard,' she appealed. 'I'm not usually so ungrateful, but I need to prove I can stand on my own feet. You have to let me try, otherwise it isn't a fair test. You said you always play fair. Do you?'

He raked long fingers through his hair, leaving trails in the ash-coloured strands. 'You seem to think I don't.'

He hadn't answered her question. Was she right, after all? The possibility disturbed her, but she had to know the truth. 'Last night, you pretended to make love to me so that I would turn and run. When it didn't work, I think you decided to try doing things for me so that I'd see how helpless I was and go home. Am I right?'

He stirred up a pile of wood chips with the toe of one boot. 'You're half-right, I came on to you last night, thinking I might persuade you to leave. But fixing your roof wasn't meant to make you feel useless. I realised what a boor I'd been and wanted to make up for it. I don't blame you for giving me a dose of my own medicine.'

Whatever was in his touch could hardly be called medicinal, she thought. It had played havoc with her senses. Just recalling the moment now set her pulse on an erratic course. Standing close to him, she could smell the earthy maleness of him undisguised by any male cosmetic. It was breathtakingly erotic.

It was an effort to speak normally. 'I'm sorry for misunderstanding you.'

'And I'm sorry I misjudged you,' he said, warmth creeping into his tone. 'Would you let me make amends by cooking dinner tonight?'

It was out before she could check herself. 'I can cook my own dinner.'

A flicker of irritation crossed his face. 'I didn't say you couldn't. Don't confuse independence with pigheadedness. You can be independent without being the whole Swiss Family Robinson, you know.'

'I know. All right, I accept your invitation.'

Much later, as she got ready to keep the appointment, she wondered why Dane had invited her to dinner. He could be sick of his own company by now, or it could be a new trick to get her to leave the island. Whichever it was, she determined to be ready. No one could accuse her of running away from a challenge.

Luckily she had located a supply of kindling wood outside her cabin, and had been able to get the stove going so that she could heat a container of rainwater for a proper wash. The soft, fragrant water left her skin feeling deliciously silken.

Now she dressed with care in a taupe linen trouser-suit which didn't look too out of place in the simple surroundings. At her throat she knotted a toning Bill Blass scarf, then fixed huge gold hoops to her ears. After seeing the way Dane dressed, she wondered if she was overdressed, but it was the closest her wardrobe came to rustic simplicity.

She needn't have worried. Dane had also dressed with care in tan cotton trousers and a cream crêpe de Chine shirt. It was casually unbuttoned, and she swallowed hard as her eye was drawn down the length of his tanned chest strewn with curling hairs which teased at the edges of the shirt. What would it be like to run her hand down that inviting expanse?

She wrenched her eyes away and met his amused gaze full on her, returning her inspection. 'You look lovely tonight.'

'Thanks.' She made her tone offhand. 'I like dressing up.'

His mouth tightened a fraction. 'Of course. You would.'

Before she could ask what she had said wrong, he turned and led the way into his cabin. It was the first time she'd been inside the other dwelling, and she was surprised at how different it was from her cabin.

It was built from local stone with an iron roof and vine-shaded back veranda. Tree trunks washed the same pale green as the house served as unusual supports for the rainwater tank at one side.

The front door opened on to a large room with a fireplace at one end. The floor was made of thick boards butted tightly together, with a scattering of rugs for warmth. Overhead, she noticed a large trapdoor which presumably led to a loft bedroom similar to her own.

'This is charming,' she enthused. 'I see you've made yourself at home here.'

'Which is precisely why I'm not eager to change the situation,' he commented. 'There isn't much more, just a lean-to kitchen and bathroom.' He opened a door to her left. 'Then there's this little room I use as a study. The place was built by a red-bearded Scottish settler. So many of his children were born in this room that it's called the Birthing Room to this day.'

She shot him a surprised glance. 'You know more about the island's history than I do.'

'It helps to be interested,' he said. Since she had no defence against the implied criticism, she swallowed her angry reaction and took the seat he pulled out for her at the table.

'The meal isn't fancy. Bouillabaisse and home-made damper. I hope you like it.'

It sounded heavenly after the cold rations she'd been eating since she'd arrived. He laughed when she said so. 'You should have told me you were having trouble with the stove. I'd have given you a hand.'

'Which is why I didn't tell you,' she said. 'I don't need looking after.'

His look said he thought differently, but he didn't argue the point. Instead, he ladled the thick seafood soup into handmade pottery bowls and cut a plate-sized round of damper for her. She sniffed at the fragrant bush bread. 'This smells wonderful. Do you enjoy cooking?'

He cut a round for himself and spread butter on it. It's a case of needs must. Janice hated cooking, so I did most of it.'

'Didn't you have staff?'

'Not after I'd finished paying her bills. What do you women do with so many dresses?'

Although she bristled at his presumption that she was as extravagant as Janice, she kept her temper. 'It depends on the life-style,' she said seriously. 'If you do a lot of charity work, you have to keep up appearances.'

'I wouldn't put charity and work in the same sentence,' he said archly.

She dropped her soup spoon with a clatter. 'Well, I would. Fund-raising can be demanding and difficult, but you can't let people starve.'

'You mean someone actually benefits from these dos?' he asked, his tone disbelieving.

'That's the general idea. I'm surprised your Janice didn't explain it to you.'

'I doubt if she was interested in the end product of her activities,' he said sourly. 'And she isn't my Janice any more. The divorce was final last Christmas.'

For some reason this lightened her mood considerably. 'Is that why you're here?' she probed.

'Yes. I needed time to sort a few things out. Janice took me for everything I owned in the end, but I could get back on my feet. I've done it before. I just don't know if I want to.'

She was aware of a change between them, as if the atmosphere had suddenly become charged with electricity. She felt the table-edge pressing against her body, a reminder that she had begun to lean towards him. It was an effort to pull back. 'What will you do now?'

'Whatever it is, I'm finished with corporate finance,' he said emphatically. 'I've started a research project here which I may decide to continue.'

'Here on the island?'

'I'm studying the Tasmanian Devil colony,' he explained. 'They're fascinating creatures when you get to know them.'

Hearing the warmth in his voice, she wondered why it vanished when he spoke about the people in his life. She found herself wondering how it would feel if he sounded so warm and caring when he spoke about her.

His pale eyes were on her, their depths inviting her to plunge in and explore the caverns of his mind. It was as if a silken cord stretched between them, linking them in some mystical way. She tried to tell herself it was the wine he had served with dinner, but she felt completely sober. The light-headed sensation she was feeling had nothing to do with alcohol.

'It's strange, but I feel as if I've known you for ages,' she said, her voice sounding as if it came from far away.

'Maybe we knew each other in another life,' he suggested lightly.

'Do you believe in such things?'

'No. But I thought you might.'

She dropped her long lashes, sheltering her eyes from his gaze. 'Don't humour me. But there is something here. Can't you feel it, too?'

For answer, he rose and came around to her side of the table. He slid his hands under her arms and urged her to her feet. Still caught up in the strange spell, she turned to find they were standing only a heartbeat apart. 'Dane?' she queried, not sure what she was asking of him.

He supplied his own question and answer. One hand slid up her back and rested against her hair. Then his arms tightened around her and his mouth took possession of hers with such delicious force that she felt as if she were being kissed for the first time. The sensation was heady and she rocked towards him, aware of the hard wall of his stomach pressing against her. She hadn't misjudged the moment. He did share her feelings.

When he lifted his head to graze her hairline with his lips, she pressed her face into his shoulder, filling her nose with the warm male scent of him. She was hardly aware that he had stopped kissing her until his hand slid inside the front of her jacket and came to rest on her breast. She almost never wore a bra, hadn't thought to do so tonight, and the touch of his work-hardened fingers against her nipple was unbelievably sensuous. She felt the rosy peak tauten, and she pushed herself further into his hand.

Being alone on the island with Dane made everything seem unreal, except the torrent of sensations waging war inside her. She tried to isolate just one of them, to understand what was happening to her. Men came and went in her life. She dated, she sailed, she partied. She didn't respond with such unbridled passion to a man—at least, she never had before. 'What's going on here?' she whispered unsteadily.

Her voice seemed to bring him back to his senses. Slowly, he withdrew his hand and refastened the top button of her jacket, then smoothed the hair back from her forehead. 'I guess we nearly ended dinner in a way neither of us planned to,' he said, the huskiness in his voice betraying the depths of his own arousal.

'How did it happen?' she asked, bemused. 'Can two people discover each other so quickly?'

His expression darkened and he went back to his side of the table, bracing himself against the back of his chair as if he needed the physical obstacles between them to say what he needed to. 'We haven't discovered anything, Evelyn. All we did was get a little turned on by the mood of the moment.'

She felt disorientated, the way she once had when she came up from a diving-expedition too fast on the Barrier Reef, and got a touch of the bends. 'Are you saying it doesn't mean anything?'

'I'm saying it can't, not this time.'

So he did feel what she felt, even if he refused to let himself acknowledge it. The thought drove some of the anger out of her. 'Why are we getting so serious?' she asked with deliberate flippancy. 'It was just a kiss, for goodness' sake. It isn't as if you were proposing marriage.'

'No, it isn't. I can't afford a woman like you, Evelyn.'

A frown studded her brow. 'I have money of my own. I'm not looking for a man to support me.'

'I didn't mean financially. I meant in my life.'

'I see.'

His pale eyes transfixed her, threatening to breach her fragile defences. 'I wonder if you do. The next woman for me, if there is one, is going to be a down-to-earth type, the kind who's happy getting a bunch of wild flowers on her birthday without looking for the diamond bracelet inside.'

A pang of guilt shot through her as she thought of the party her father had staged for her last birthday. The papers reported the cost at a million dollars, although the reality was more like six hundred thousand. Charlton had flown a chef and his entire staff from Canberra to Hobart for the occasion and had chartered the city's finest restaurant for the night.

With the guilt came anger that Dane should judge her so harshly for doing what was, after all, no more than enjoy her blessings. What right had he to say that was wrong? 'I don't know why you're getting so hot under the collar,' she said, hearing her voice vibrant with rage. 'I didn't come here looking for a man, either. Just the opposite, in fact. There are plenty of men who'd love to put the world at my feet. I happen to have plans other than to submerge myself in a man's ego.'

Take that, she thought furiously. Dane Balkan wasn't having it all his way. To her astonishment, she saw that he was smiling, although his eyes remained cold and assessing. 'Good,' he said shortly. 'I'm glad we understand each other.'

But they didn't, did they? He had made his feelings clear, but she wasn't sure what her feelings were, except that she reacted more powerfully to him than to any other man she had ever met.

CHAPTER FOUR

EVELYN cast a critical eye over the garden surrounding her cabin. What a difference she had made to it since she had arrived. The dense covering of Anodopetalum—known locally as 'horizontal' because of the way it grew—had been cleared from two sides of the cabin. Hacking it away, she had uncovered some beautiful tree ferns which now took pride of place in her newly created rain-forest garden.

She pushed the hair back from her eyes with a grubby hand, wincing at the sight of her chipped nails. Could this be the same Evelyn Consett who had stepped off Ned Freils' boat unable even to light a wood-burning stove? Not only could she do it with ease now, she had chopped a pile of logs to replace those she'd used. They were inexpertly done and very ragged-looking, but she was proud of them nevertheless. Yesterday she had even tried her hand at baking damper using Dane's recipe. She was becoming quite a pioneer woman.

A low groan escaped her lips as she straightened and leaned on her spade, feeling her back muscles protesting. Maybe moving those bush rocks hadn't been such a smart idea. Dane would gladly have done it for her. He called every day to see how she was doing. Only her own stubbornness had prevented her from seeking his help.

The phone rang inside the cabin. She now knew that Dane didn't have a telephone in his cottage, relying on the radio aboard his motorboat for contact with the outside world, so the caller must be from the mainland. Probably her father, she thought with a sigh of resignation. She dropped the spade and swung towards the house, drawing a sharp breath as her strained muscles pained her.

But it wasn't her father. 'It's me, Julie,' came her friend's cheerful voice. 'Did I interrupt anything important?'

The conspiratorial way she dropped her voice made Evelyn aware that Julie assumed someone was with her on the island. 'You didn't interrupt anything,' she said firmly. 'I was working in the garden.'

'You, gardening?' Julie's tone was sceptical. 'Next thing you'll be telling me you're enjoying this crazy experiment.'

'As a matter of fact, I am. I've lost four pounds and worked up a sensational tan.' She didn't add that her hair was a mess and her hands looked as if they belonged to a farm labourer. Oddly, such details no longer seemed as important as they had done a week ago.

'Maybe I should give this self-sufficiency thing a try,' Julie suggested. 'I could do with losing some weight myself.'

'You're welcome to join me,' Evelyn offered, knowing that her friend's idea of roughing it was to turn off her electric blanket.

'Thanks, but no thanks.' Julie sounded faintly alarmed at being taken seriously, even for a minute.

'Actually, I rang to lure you away from your island paradise.'

Thinking of her father, Evelyn grimaced at the phone. 'You aren't the first to try, but it won't work. I'm not leaving till the end of the month. Then my father will have to admit that I'm not the hothouse flower he thinks I am.'

'You aren't serious about going to work for him, are you? I thought this was just a joke.'

'Well, it isn't. I'm more serious than I've ever been about anything.'

'Then you won't come back for Jerry's thirtieth birthday party?' Julie sounded distressed. 'We were counting on you.'

'We' meant Jerry Cummings, Julie's brother, Evelyn knew. He made no secret of his interest in her. They had gone out together a few times, often enough for Evelyn to realise how shallow and selfish he really was. Ironically, her father considered Jerry a perfect match for his daughter.

'He's one of the Battery Point Cummings,' he had reminded her when she criticised Jerry. 'They're very big in iron and steel.'

'Dad, you make it sound like a merger,' she protested. 'I don't like his company. Doesn't that count?'

His frown was ominous. 'In a family like ours, marriage *is* a kind of merger, an alliance of complementary interests, if you will. We're like royalty, m'girl. We have to give careful thought to your future partner.'

'We?' she thought with a slight stirring of hysteria. She had foolishly imagined that she would marry for love. That was when the idea of embarking on a career and some measure of independence had occurred to her. She felt driven to show her father that she was an individual, not a commodity to be traded when he judged it opportune.

'So what do you say, will you come? You can go back to your island straight after the party,' Julie urged, breaking into her thoughts.

'I'm sorry, I can't,' she repeated, knowing that her father would love an excuse to break their agreement. 'Wish Jerry a happy birthday for me.'

'OK, but you're missing the party of the year.'

They exchanged goodbyes and Evelyn hung up. Strangely enough, she didn't feel any regrets about missing the party. It would be the usual all-night do with a famous band being paid a fortune to be ignored by the sons and daughters of the élite. Julie would no doubt provoke someone into pushing her into the swimming-pool so that she would have the excuse to parade her fabulous figure in a dripping dress that clung to every curve. Most of her clothes looked better wet than dry, and Evelyn smiled as she realised this was no accident.

Jerry would have a few drinks and pretend to be drunker than he really was, so that he could corner some unsuspecting girl, then afterwards blame his behaviour on the drink.

A shudder shook her as she realised that this had been her idea of fun, too, until recently. What had made her change?

All this working in the open air had something to do with it, she thought with a wry smile. She pressed a fist into the small of her back, kneading her sore muscles. She was going to feel like hell in the morning.

Hell was an understatement, she realised when she awoke next day. Every muscle in her body screamed a painful protest as she tried to straighten out. Even after the most strenuous aerobics class, she had never endured such agony as this afterwards.

It was all she could do to sit up and bring her feet to the floor. The tears flooding her eyes told her it wasn't going to work. There was no way she could manage the stairs and cook breakfast for herself. All she wanted was to lie back and rest her aching body.

No position was really comfortable, and every move brought a fresh wave of pain. It was a miracle that she managed to fall asleep again.

The sun was high in the sky by the time she stirred, groaning as pain flooded back into her limbs, making her want to retreat into sleep again. But the voice calling her name refused to let her retreat. She whimpered as she tried to sit up. It sounded like Dane. 'I'm up here,' she called out weakly.

From the brief creaking of the stair treads, she guessed he had taken them two at the time. How wonderful to be so fit and agile, she thought enviously.

Then the door sprang open, and Dane's pale gaze took in her huddled form. 'What's the matter? Are you ill?' he demanded. His tone was rough, as if he was trying not to reveal any concern for her beyond what was expected of a good neighbour.

She forced a laugh. 'You could say that. I think I damaged some muscles making the rock garden yesterday.'

Annoyance darkened his eyes to that of the sky on a stormy day. 'What the hell were you doing, shoving rocks around, anyway?'

She flinched from his anger. 'Don't yell at me. How was I to know I'd feel like this after a bit of exercise?'

'That's not exercise. It's weight-lifting. You should have called me if you wanted to rearrange the landscape.'

'I wanted to do it myself.' She couldn't understand why he was so angry. Then she had it. His macho pride was dented because she hadn't asked for his help. 'I can do things for myself, you know.'

His generous mouth tightened into a grim line. 'So I see. Is that why you're still in bed at two in the afternoon?'

Her eyes widened. 'Is it as late as that?' No wonder she felt ravenous. She had slept the clock around.

He nodded. 'I don't suppose you've had any food either.'

She shook her head. 'I decided I needed rest more than food.'

'Lying there is the worst thing you could do. What you need is to get those muscles working again.'

She rolled her eyes expressively. 'The man is trying to kill me.'

'No, I'm not. Trust me. I've been through this.'

A vivid memory of his naked body as he bathed in the waterfall sprang into her mind. The flawless mahogany tan had revealed rock-hard muscles which could never have troubled him as hers were doing now. He looked the picture of physical perfection.

He saw the doubt on her face. 'It's true. When I came here a couple of months ago, I was a desk worker. Sure, I swam a lot and worked out at a gymnasium, but I didn't realise how selective those kinds of exercise were until I really started to make demands on my body.'

'So what did you do?'

'The same thing I'm going to do for you. A long hot soak in a deep bath, then a massage and a hot meal. You'll feel quite differently in an hour or so, I promise.'

She was sure she would, she thought, feeling the colour surge into her face. Instinctively, she pulled the bedclothes up under her chin. Already, Dane Balkan had made dangerous inroads into her quest for independence. Letting him get any closer was madness. 'You can run the bath for me,' she compromised. 'But I'll take a raincheck on everything else.'

'Bath first, then see how you feel,' he said, his face expressionless.

With a feeling of relief, she heard him go downstairs and into the lean-to bathroom next to the kitchen. Then came the roaring and popping sounds of the chip heater being lit. Dane seemed to find it much easier than she did. One bath in three had been lukewarm since she arrived, because the wretched heater refused to stay alight.

She sighed. A warm bath sounded like heaven right now. After having to do every little thing for herself since she came here, it would be wonderful to let someone else do the work while she settled back to enjoy it.

A prickly sensation like a warning crept over her, blotting out some of her aches. She couldn't lie back and enjoy his touch, whatever the temptation. She had to remember that they were both here to cut their ties, not to create new ones.

Dane seemed to have no trouble remembering it. His touch was impersonal as he helped her out of bed and down the stairs to the bathroom. Every step was agony, and she bit her lip to stop herself from crying aloud.

'You can yell if you want to,' he told her, noticing her efforts to remain stoic.

'I'm fine, really,' she lied. Letting herself go was something she hadn't had much practice at doing. She was better versed in keeping up appearances, no matter how much pain there was behind the façade. It was hard to remember that they were alone on an island and society's rules didn't have to apply.

'I can see you are,' he said sarcastically. 'But have it your own way.'

She let him help her off with her dressing-gown, but resisted when he reached for her nightdress. Already she was achingly aware of him in a way she had no business being. 'I can manage,' she insisted.

He shrugged as if he didn't care either way. 'I'll be in the kitchen if you need me. Enjoy your bath.'

She waited until he had closed the door before she hoisted the long nightdress over her head. She wore nothing underneath, so it took her only another minute to step into the claw-footed bathtub and sink up to her neck in the blissfully hot water.

Dane had added something to the water, she discovered, as the fragrance of herbs teased her nostrils. It was probably some concoction to ease her muscles, she decided. Maybe it had been in the bathroom all along without her realising its purpose. Whatever it was, it was bliss to lie there while the knots in her body gradually loosened and the sharp pains diminished to bearable aches.

'Don't go to sleep in there.'

She forced her heavy lids open and became aware that Dane was standing over the tub, looking down at her. She must have been on the verge of dozing off, because she hadn't heard him come in. She was thankful that the herbal concoction had coloured the water, shielding her from his gaze.

Not that he seemed in the least disturbed by the sight of her lying in the bath. She felt a twinge of annoyance that she apparently wasn't attractive enough to arouse him. Then she chided herself for the thought. The last thing she needed was another take-charge man in her life. Hadn't she learned anything from her father?

'Feeling better?' he asked when he saw that she was fully awake.

'Much better, thank you,' she said primly. 'You needn't keep watch over me. I'll be out in a minute.'

A flicker of irritation darkened his even features. For a moment, she could have sworn that he wasn't as unmoved as he seemed. But then, the moisture filming his brow could easily be caused by the steamy atmosphere in the bathroom, couldn't it?

He left without a word and she looked after him speculatively. Her body felt hot, the nerve-endings sensitised to a degree that she had never experienced before. It had to be the effects of the bath. Yet she couldn't deny that Dane's presence had done something to her as well. She made up her mind to thank him for the bath and send him back to his own cabin before things got out of hand.

But he had other ideas. When she joined him in the kitchen, her robe belted securely around her, she saw that he had covered the massive wooden table with a folded blanket. 'I'm ready for you. Hop up,' he instructed.

She was besieged by conflicting sensations—of wanting his touch and being afraid of the consequences. The wanting won. 'You'll have to turn your back,' she said huskily.

With a sigh of impatience he did so, and she slipped out of her robe, then lay face-down on the table. 'I'm ready,' she said, her voice muffled by the blanket.

'Where does it hurt?' he asked.

She tried to cast him in the role of a chiropractor she had once visited, when too much tennis had taken a toll of her arm and shoulder muscles.

Her hand moved over her back, indicating a spot low down on her hips. 'The worst ache is around there.'

Despite her best efforts, her voice came out more vibrant than she wanted it to. Why couldn't she be as impersonal as he was, taking the benefits he was offering without complicating matters?

It was easier said than done, she discovered when he laid his hands on the small of her back and began working the muscles on either side of her spine. At first, the pain of the movement blotted out everything else, then gradually her muscles relaxed and the warmth spread throughout her body. The pressure of his fingers was a delicious invasion as he sought out each aching muscle and coaxed it to unknot.

It came as a surprise to discover that the relaxation had vanished, replaced by a quivering sense of anticipation which made her stomach muscles constrict and her breathing quicken. She knew she should tell him to stop, but the words refused to come. She didn't want them to come, she realised. She wanted him to go on touching her like this forever.

With a sense of shock, she felt him drape a towel over her. She clutched at it as a drowning person might clutch a lifeline, and swathed it around herself as she sat up. Dane hadn't said a word since he finished, and she was afraid to meet his eyes, knowing that she was the only one the moment had affected.

But she wasn't, she found out when she finally mustered the courage to face him. His sculptured features were flushed and his breathing was every bit as laboured as hers. It could be the effort of massaging her, but somehow she knew it wasn't.

As he looked at her his pale eyes held a strange light.

Slowly, he curved his hands around her neck, drawing her close to him. She moved like a sleep-walker until their faces were on a level, then he traced a thumb over her jawline and along the cleft of her chin, until it met the moistness of her parted lips. Hungrily, she pressed them against his thumb.

The gesture was enough to snap his remaining control. Gathering her against him, he found her mouth and claimed it with his own, driving the breath out of her body.

All the reasons why they should remain aloof from each other, so important a moment ago, now seemed not to matter a whit. All that mattered was for Dane to go on kissing her with urgent passion. It was the pressure against her thigh which finally brought her to her senses. 'This is crazy,' she breathed as her vision cleared.

He regained his senses slowly. 'You're right. It isn't what we came here for, is it?'

Her senses were in chaos and it was an effort to speak normally. 'No, it wasn't.'

'You'd better get dressed. I'll get some more wood for the stove.'

Since she had replenished the wood box last night, it was a blatant excuse to get away from her. She understood his need to put some distance be-tween them. She felt the same way. So she merely nodded agreement.

When he had gone outside, she remained where she was on the table, her legs dangling over the side, reliving the last few minutes. The pressure of his mouth was still fresh on hers, and her body quivered with awareness of the arousal she had created in him. She had no doubt now that his need had been every bit as great as her own. The thought of how close they had just come to assuaging that need sent a wave of heat pouring through her body.

She tried to tell herself it was simply the heat of the moment, that it meant nothing. Dane had made himself perfectly clear. He wanted no part of her life, or of her, for that matter. She belonged in the same despised category as his ex-wife.

And she wasn't about to exchange the bonds of life with her father for a similar role as someone's wife.

It was crazy to let things get so far out of hand. Letting herself get involved with Dane was asking for trouble when there was no future in it for either of them.

By the time he returned with an armful of firewood, she was composed again. She had used his absence to dress in jeans and a bulky cable-knit sweater, well aware that she had chosen the voluminous garment to hide herself from him, although what good that would do, she wasn't sure. Beneath the thick sweater, her skin felt prickly and sensitive, as if his touch had electrified her.

Piling the wood on top of what was already there, Dane grinned. 'At least you won't run out for a while.'

By unspoken agreement, they reverted to their old relationship of 'good neighbours'. It was a sham and he knew it as well as she did, but if they were to last the month together on the island they had to pretend.

'Was there a reason for your visit today?' she asked him in a brittle tone.

He indicated a blackened kettle on top of her stove. 'I brought you some home-made soup, since you liked my bouillabaisse so much.'

She felt an urgent need to keep him here, although she recognised she was playing with fire. 'In that case, I hope you'll share it with me.'

His sharp gaze raked her, telling her he was aware of her tactic. To her relief, he nodded. 'I'd like that.'

'I made some damper yesterday. It's not as good as yours, but I think it's edible,' she said.

She got out the rounded loaf, thankful that at least one batch had turned out the way it was supposed to. The others had all sunk in the middle, instead of rising and turning invitingly golden.

She cut chunks for them both, and placed butter in the centre of the table, feeling her colour heighten as she recalled her behaviour on that same table a short time ago.

Dane seemed not to notice. He ladled the soup into bowls and brought it to the table, then sat down opposite her. 'At least you're feeling better,' he observed, bending his head over his meal.

She had been so preoccupied that she had almost forgotten her aching muscles, she realised with surprise. Some therapy, she thought ruefully. It wasn't something you could teach at medical school. A change of subject was urgently indicated. 'How is the research going?' she asked.

'I've amassed a lot of data on the Tasmanian Devil colony. They're becoming quite tame.' He leaned towards her. 'Tell me, what would you think of turning the island into a sanctuary for the animals?'

Still caught up in her own thoughts and response, she gave him a startled look. 'You mean, stop people coming here?'

'No, I mean turn the cabins into visitors' centres where people can come and learn about the animals, instead of just spending holidays here as they do now.'

She examined the idea thoughtfully. 'Under the terms of the legacy, I can't sell the island, but there's nothing to stop me turning it into a wildlife sanctuary.' Another tantalising thought occurred to her. 'Would you live here and run it?'

'Probably not,' he said, dashing her hopes. 'You'd need someone with a lot more experience in park management and animal husbandry.'

Her disappointment was thinly masked. 'I thought . . .'

'You thought you could keep me here like some sort of pet, for your amusement,' he cut in, his tone harsh. 'I should have seen it coming.'

'I didn't mean it like that,' she said, her voice tremulous. She felt ashamed, because she had been thinking something of the sort and realised how unworthy it was. 'I thought, because it was your idea, you'd like to help establish the reserve.'

'Then I'm sorry if I jumped to conclusions,' he said gruffly. 'But I'm the wrong man, believe me.'

She had a feeling he was telling her more than his words indicated. He was reminding her that he wanted no part of her life. It was a lesson she would do well to take to heart.

'All the same, I like the idea,' she ventured, trying to recapture his goodwill. 'My mother would have liked it too, since she loved coming here.'

'Your mother was a painter, wasn't she?' Dane said, surprising her. 'I've seen her work in charity shows.'

'That's right. She believed she wasn't good enough to exhibit professionally, so she donated her paintings to charities. I have one of her water-colours in my bedroom at home. It was done here, but I don't know where. Are there any caves on the island?'

'Only one that I know of,' Dane supplied. 'It's known as the Friar's Cave. He used to live there, I believe.'

'Is that why the place is known as Frere Island, after the monk?'

'He was a Franciscan friar actually, and he only had one arm. He lived in the cave and fed the ani-mals, which is why there are so many of them today.'

'What happened to him?'

'According to the legend, he was out in a boat when the hook he used as his right arm got tangled in the anchor chain. The falling anchor pulled him overboard. His ghost is said to haunt the cave.'

She shivered. 'What a terrible story. Luckily, I don't believe in ghosts.'

His gaze on her was soft. 'What do you believe in?'

You, she thought, feeling a knot of tension swell in her breast. How would he react to such a confession? She knew perfectly well. He would remind her that it was futile. And he'd be right. So she made her tone light as she said, 'I believe in having a good time, enjoying yourself. Living for today, all that jazz.'

The derision in his eyes struck her like a physical blow. 'I should have known.'

She felt moved to defend herself. 'Is it so wrong?'

'Given your upbringing, I suppose not.'

Anger made her want to lash out at him, to ask him what he expected her to say. If she admitted to sharing his concerns, he wouldn't believe her anyway. 'Whatever you say,' she conceded in a tone of defeat.

He stood up. 'It's almost sunset. I'd better be getting back to feed the animals. I'll give you a hand to clear up.'

'No, leave them. Doing the dishes will help me pass the time.' And stop her thinking too much about him, she thought, although she recognised it was a faint hope.

He gripped the back of the chair with such force that his knuckles whitened. He seemed to be fighting some sort of battle with himself. 'I've got a better idea,' he said suddenly. 'Why don't you come back with me, to my cabin?'

CHAPTER FIVE

THE SUDDENNESS of his request caught her off balance as she licked her dry lips, trying to marshal her whirling thoughts. Her expensive education had equipped her to handle most situations with grace and tact, but neither was appropriate to deal with such a blatant invitation. 'I don't know,' she murmured, speaking the absolute truth.

'I thought you wanted to see me feed the animals,' he observed. 'This is the perfect chance.'

As she felt the colour creep up her face, she started busily clearing away the dishes. What an idiot she was, imagining that he had meant something more. 'I don't think so,' she said gruffly, keeping her face averted.

Something in her voice alerted him. He moved to her side and cupped her chin in one strong hand, drawing her around to face him. 'You sound disappointed. Is something the matter?'

At his touch, a shudder passed through her slender body. 'Of course not.'

His eyes narrowed to slits, the light in them as pale yet penetrating as the moonlight outside. They seemed to see into her very soul. 'You weren't reading too much into my invitation just now?'

She forced a laugh. 'Should I?'

'Maybe.'

His hand travelled from her chin to the side of her neck, where it rested like a caress. 'Then maybe we'd better forget about the animals,' she said huskily.

He dropped his hand and moved back a pace. 'You're probably right.' This time, he was the one who sounded disappointed.

She waited until she heard the door close behind him, then she went to the window and looked out. His impressive frame was rimmed by an aura of moonlight, so that every feature glowed with the vitality and power she had come to associate with him. The aura began to fade as his long strides took him deeper into the bush, away from her.

Fighting an almost overpowering urge to call him back, she bustled around the cabin, putting things away and plumping up cushions. When she came to the one where his back had rested, she grazed her hand over the hollow, a dreamy smile spreading over her face.

It was quickly replaced by a feeling of dismay. What had happened to her precious quest for independence? How her father would laugh if he could see her mooning over a man like this, and not from one of the Battery Point families at that. A laugh that was half a sob shook her. Dane was right. They were about as ill suited as two people could be.

She was still telling herself this as she snatched up her crocheted wrap and hurtled out of the door.

Although she flew down the path on winged feet, Dane had already begun to feed the Tasmanian Devils by the time she reached his cabin.

She paused on the edge of the clearing, not wanting to disturb the animals. She doubted whether they would have heard her over the noise of their feeding, but she decided to be cautious.

Clustered around Dane were a dozen animals, ranging from cat-size to the size of a fox terrier—depending on age, she assumed. They were all covered in coarse black fur with jagged patches of white around their necks. From the snapping of their powerful jaws to the occasional growls and squeals which punctuated their feeding, she would have thought they were fighting. But, since Dane made no move to intervene, she guessed this must be their normal behaviour.

He bent down and ruffled the neck of one creature. 'Hey, Henrietta, leave some for the others.'

So that was Henrietta, the destroyer of her supplies. She smiled, remembering how she had accused Dane of the deed. The little scamp at his feet looked much more capable of such mischief.

'Are they tame enough to approach?' she called softly.

Dane's head snapped up and he noticed her at the edge of the clearing. 'So you decided to come, after all.'

She began to circle around the feeding animals. 'I didn't seem to be able to stay away.'

'You can come closer. They won't hurt you.'

But what about Dane himself? she wondered as she moved to his side. He was a Tasmanian Devil in his own right, every bit as fierce and elusive as the creatures at their feet. He had one more characteristic in common with them. He was determined never to seek a mate outside his own kind again.

All the same, she couldn't suppress the rush of pleasure she felt at the sight of his big, capable hands gently separating a pair of squabbling animals, or apportioning meat from a bin into the smaller plates from which the Devils were feeding.

A vision of Dane, surrounded by a cluster of tawny-haired children, popped into her mind, but she chased it away. 'Can I help?' she asked, diverting her thoughts back to where they belonged.

He passed the bin to her. 'It's chopped chicken. They're strictly meat-eaters.'

'With those teeth, I'm not surprised.'

They spent the next half-hour making sure that all the animals got their fair share of food, and refereeing the disagreements which broke out every so often. Dane explained that Tasmanian Devils were aggressive by nature, at least with each other. But despite their fierce appearance, he said, they had trouble killing a rat and could themselves be killed by a dog.

'If the dingo had reached Tasmania, the Devils would probably be extinct here too, as they are in the rest of Australia,' he added.

She gave the last piece of chicken to Henrietta, and showed the empty bin to the other Tasmanian Devils waiting hopefully nearby. Finally realising that the feast was over, they began to melt back into the bush. 'Is that why you're so keen to set up a sanctuary here, because they're so rare?' she asked Dane.

'They're not rare at all,' he contradicted her. 'These days, you can find them all over Tasmania, even in some of the suburbs. But very few are tame, even in the sanctuaries which already exist. I like the idea that children can come here, see them close up but still in their natural surroundings, and get to know them better. I grew up with animals on my family's farm, and it concerns me that children today think that milk grows in glass bottles.'

'All this is a long way from the Stock Exchange,' she said.

He grew serious. 'It can't be far enough for me.'

She rested the empty food bin on her knees and crossed her arms over the top. 'Why did you go into high finance if you dislike it so much?'

'In our society, money is power. It gives you the freedom to do what you want with your life. I realised that if I wanted that freedom I would have to go where the money was, at least for a time.'

'I understand,' she said, nodding thoughtfully.

He combed his hair with splayed fingers. 'I wish Janice had understood. She accused me of giving up just when I was becoming successful. She didn't understand that my work was a means to an end.'

In spite of herself, she was curious. 'Where is she now?'

'Married to a retail tycoon in Melbourne.'

It explained why their paths hadn't crossed, she thought. Something in the intimacy of the night gave her the assurance to ask, 'Do you still love her?'

'No. What love we thought we had didn't last past the three months it took me to find out that

I'd married a china doll, a beautiful facade. There was nothing of substance underneath.'

Hearing him talk like this made her feel as if she, and not his ex-wife, were the person being disparaged. 'Did you take the time to look?' she asked, her tranquil mood swallowed up by annoyance.

'Of course I did. I tried to talk things over with her, but every opinion she had came from her tutors at her fancy finishing-school, not from her own beliefs.'

'I'm surprised you care about anyone else's opinions,' she shot back. 'Janice couldn't help being what she was. If her family was like mine, she was brought up to sit quietly, look decorative and forget having a mind of your own.'

The look he gave her was filled with grudging respect.

'In your case, the lesson evidently didn't take.'

Some of her anger subsided. He couldn't know it, but he had just paid her a compliment. 'I thought all families were the same,' she went on. 'I only rebelled when my father starting talking about marrying me off as if I were a family asset.'

'Oh, you're definitely that,' he said, his tone deep and caressing. 'But it still amounts to coming here because you didn't get your own way.'

The flame of anger which had begun to burn lower flared again. 'Why do you twist my words? If I weren't a lady, I'd . . .'

'Go on,' he prompted, his eyes flashing a challenge. 'What would you do?'

The feed bin rolled away as she jumped to her feet. She was about to launch herself at Dane when a small voice intruded, dredged up from her schooldays. 'A lady remains composed, no matter what the provocation.' She sat down again. 'Nothing.'

In the light spilling from the cabin door, his smile was cynically twisted. 'That's what I expected. Just when I think a real person is about to emerge, you retreat behind that polished façade.'

Just like Janice, was the unspoken conclusion. 'I am a real person,' she protested. 'Just because I was well brought up...'

He slashed a hand through the air, the gesture cutting her off in mid-sentence. 'Well brought up, be damned. You were packaged. Your manners, clothes, hair, even your small talk is part of the packaging.'

Another thought occurred to her and it was out before she could stop it, petty though it was. 'You're jealous of me because of my background, aren't you?'

'Not jealous, contemptuous.'

It was said with such intensity that she couldn't help believing it. All thoughts of good manners and decorum were swept aside in a rush of anger which engulfed her. With a little animal cry, she flew at him. 'What do you know about my life, you smug pirate? I hate you, I hate...'

He caught her upraised fists and held them away from him as easily as he had held the Tasmanian Devils apart earlier. As she subsided into sobs, he brought her close to him and cradled her against his chest. If he knew she had begun to say 'I hate me,' he gave no sign but merely made soothing sounds as he stroked her hair over and over.

'There, it's all right. Go ahead and let it out, it will do you good.'

They were the sort of sounds one might make to a distraught child, but she couldn't have cared less as she clung to him, giving vent to years of frustration and discontent. Finally, the storm spent itself and she collapsed against his chest, grateful for the feel of his strong arms around her.

Gradually, she became aware of the rhythmic beating of his heart under her cheek. It was a powerful sound, strong and resilient, as if it would go on forever. She was unaware of nestling closer until his hold tightened. 'Oh, Dane,' she murmured.

Of their own accord, her arms crept up around his neck and she clasped her fingers together. The pressure drew his head towards her and she tilted her face back, her lips parted expectantly.

His response was swift and unerring as he claimed her mouth and plundered it with his eager, seeking tongue. The contact seared her to the core and her body arched against him.

His breathing became fast and ragged as he slid a knee in between hers. As she tightened her thighs around it, she heard him gasp with surprised pleasure. His hands roved through her hair, twining curls around his fingers, as the kiss deepened.

After what seemed an age, he withdrew his mouth long enough to whisper, 'You know I want you, Evelyn. I've wanted you since the moment we met.'

'I know,' she said, hearing her voice come out husky with desire. The very thought of what the night might bring was enough to set her senses on fire, and every nerve quivered with excitement. 'But I thought you hated me.'

'Hate is the other side of the coin called love. I don't hate you, Evelyn. Never that.'

With her head cradled against his shoulder, she looked up at him with troubled eyes. 'Never?'

'Not now, not like this.'

A vague feeling of disquiet rippled through her, warring with the magic of being in his arms. He didn't hate her when she was his pioneer woman, helping him feed the wild animals and tilling the soil till her fingernails splintered. But what about when she was Evelyn Consett, belle of the ball?

The heat of his kiss drove all doubts out of her head, and she found herself responding with a passion she didn't know she possessed. He began to move, the restless stirring barely noticeable until she felt herself catching fire. Forcing her heavy eyelids open, she saw that her quivering response had ignited his. His eyes were flame, their paleness consumed by desire for her. She had never known she had such power.

His hot breath whispered across her cheeks. 'Now, my darling?'

'Yes, Dane. Oh, yes.'

He helped her to her feet, and they trod the golden path of light into his cabin. She felt like a sleepwalker, participating in a beautiful dream which commanded all her senses.

She was surprised when he steered her into the living-room instead of towards the staircase leading to the loft bedroom. 'It's warmer in here,' he said, in answer to her questioning look.

In the living-room, a fire blazed in the fireplace, the flames leaping orange-red to disappear up the chimney in a shower of golden sparks. Entranced, she watched it while he unrolled a huge fur rug in front of the hearth. 'Here, my love,' he said, guiding her on to it.

Even through the thickness of her sweater, the rug felt luxurious and soft and she lay back on it, her head resting in the crook of Dane's arm. His gaze, which never left her, was as heated as the firelight. She basked in its warmth.

With exquisite tenderness, he slid her sweater up and caressed her breasts, cupping each one in turn, then bending his head to it. When his teeth grazed each sensitive peak, her back arched and a low moan reached her ears. Distantly, she realised the sound came from her own throat. When he eased the sweater over her head, it was a relief to be free of the restrictive garment. She wanted him to have his fill of every part of her, sure that unless he did she would explode into flames of unfulfilled desire.

But the moment of fulfilment was not quite yet. When she could take no more of his sweet torment, he allowed her to slake some of her thirst by exploring his body as she would. She found it exciting and satisfying all at once, never having been given the freedom of a man's body before. The men she had known socially—boys, as they seemed now by comparison with Dane—took more than they gave, never taking her needs into account. To have a lover consider her so fully, in the midst of his own all-too-apparent arousal, was miraculous. She felt moved to tears.

He brushed the wetness from her cheek with the back of one finger. 'What's this? I haven't hurt you in any way, have I?'

She smiled at her own foolishness. 'No, they're tears of happiness, that's all.'

'So soon? I haven't begun to make you happy.'

His words, so rich with promise, started the laughter bubbling in her throat. Sharing her laughter, Dane gathered her into his arms and buried his head in her hair. She could feel his shoulders shaking with pointless, joyous mirth.

Suddenly there was no time for laughter or tears. As one, they sat up and began to shed their remaining clothes, tearing buttons and snagging zippers in their giddy downhill race for possession of each other. When it finally came, it was like the moment of take-off from a ski-jump, followed by the soaring, unfettered joy of being airborne. They were one in their surging, soaring passion, the ebb and flow irresistible in its thrusting power. Breathless, she went with Dane to the very brink of the ski-jump, before they soared together on a last, glorious slalom of desire. Then the ground came rushing up to meet them, blurring as the world gathered speed beneath them.

Afterwards, they lay entwined, watching the dancing flames with the complacency of those whose own fire is gloriously quenched. Evelyn was aware of Dane murmuring in her ear, but the words mattered less than the soothing sound of his voice and the comforting feel of his arms about her.

She was unaware of drifting into sleep until she awoke to find the fire burnt low. Morning sunshine spilled across the floor, stopping at her side as if in homage. She had never felt so contented before.

During the night Dane had covered her with a blanket, and she pulled it up under her chin, luxuriating in the blissful warmth. There was a pillow under her head, too, where last night there had been Dane's arms. The switch caused her a twinge of regret.

A feeling of alarm soon followed as she realised that Dane was no longer beside her. Hearing him pottering around in the kitchen, she relaxed again. All was right with the world.

'Wake up, sleepyhead,' he said, coming into the room.

Tucking the rug under her arms, she sat upright and accepted the steaming mug of coffee he held out. She wrapped her hands around it, enjoying the warmth radiating from it. 'And a good morning to you, too,' she said. 'How long have you been awake?'

'Oh, since dawn,' he said, then relented. 'I've only been up a few minutes.' He stretched and groaned. 'I'm stiff from sleeping on that floor, but otherwise, I feel fine.'

Her eyes flashed challenging fire. 'Only fine? I feel like taking on the world.'

'In that case, you can chop the firewood,' he said with a grin. 'And I'll know just what to do next time the supplies run low.'

'Oh, you!' She put the coffee-mug down long enough to aim her pillow at him, but he ducked and it sailed harmlessly past. 'I only came here to feed the Tasmanian Devils,' she said ruefully.

'You called me a devil more than once,' he reminded her. 'And you know what they say about living by bread alone?'

Since she had no more pillows to throw at him, she contented herself with pulling a face. 'Just as well you brought me the coffee so I can't be too hard on you. But breakfast had better be good.'

As soon as she saw his jaw muscles tighten with disapproval, she knew she'd said the wrong thing. 'Is that an order?' he asked, his tone deceptively soft.

His sudden change of mood set alarm bells ringing in her mind. 'Of course it isn't,' she hastened to say. 'I was joking. You know—ha, ha?'

'Yes, very funny,' he agreed, but remained tight-lipped. 'I suppose you have breakfast in bed every morning at home.'

'Not every morning,' she contradicted, failing to see his trap. 'Most days, Sarah only brings me my coffee, then I have muesli and juice downstairs. Oh, for goodness' sake! You make me sound thoroughly spoiled.'

'You said it,' he rejoined.

She lifted her hands in surrender, but inwardly she felt shaken. She remembered Dane's rule not to get involved with another wealthy woman. She felt as if his comments just now were designed to remind her of that. 'Well, you don't need to worry,' she said, disguising her pain with light humour. 'I don't expect my lovers to bring me breakfast. I usually do the cooking.'

Her careful choice of words, like 'lovers', plural, and 'usually', had their intended effect. Under the rich tan, Dane's face paled and his eyes narrowed. 'I see. Just as long as I know.'

Saying he had work to do outside, he left her to dress and make the promised breakfast. But it was a long time before she moved the blanket aside and rolled to her feet. Already she regretted giving Dane the idea that last night was the kind of thing she did often. In fact, the very opposite was true.

In her twenty-four years, there had only been one serious love in her life. He was a fellow university student, and their affair had been as intense as it was brief. It lasted only until her father found out and offered the young man a lucrative job in the Northern Territory, about as far from his daughter as could be arranged.

Her love for Michael had died with his capitulation to her father's wishes. Thinking of it now, she couldn't blame him for making the most of a golden opportunity. No doubt he had meant it when he'd said he would send for her as soon as he was established. It wasn't his fault that he had fallen in love with someone else up there. At least he had the courage to write and tell Evelyn it was over, instead of leaving her to wonder.

It probably wouldn't have worked anyway, she thought with a sigh. These days, she had trouble recalling what Michael looked like.

She was dressed in her sweater and jeans, and had her blankets neatly rolled up by the time Dane returned with an armful of firewood. 'This should be enough for breakfast,' he said, without looking at her.

Tentatively, she touched his sleeve, drawing his gaze to her. 'Look, I didn't mean what I said before, about making breakfast for all my lovers. This is not how I usually behave at all.'

His eyebrows rose fractionally. 'Making breakfast or making love?' he asked.

She whirled away from him, anger sparking through her. 'Do you have to be so hateful?'

He caught up with her at the window, pressing his hands on to her shoulders so that she was forced to turn around. He kept his hands in place, trapping her between his arms. 'I don't want to hurt you, Evelyn. I just want you to understand that this can't go any further.'

'And what you want, you usually get, right?' she asked, her voice shaky.

For a heart-stopping moment, he stood looking down at her, his gaze translucent. 'That's what I thought,' he forced out. 'But maybe not this time.'

Before she could ask what he meant, he slid his hands around her back and clasped her to him. Instinctively she tilted her head back and ran her tongue over her lips, moistening them in invitation.

The gesture elicited a groan from him, then he bent his head and kissed her with fierce possessiveness. Memories of last night's intimacies stirred in her body and she moved restlessly against him. She felt the answering stirring in him and her legs went weak. It would be so easy to succumb, so very easy.

From deep in her mind came the reminder that this was all he could offer her. He wanted no part of the rest of Evelyn Consett. She pushed her flattened palms against his muscular chest.

His hold slackened and he looked at her from beneath heavy eyelids. 'What is it?'

'I don't want you to make love to me,' she insisted, trying to make the lie sound convincing. She did want him to make love to her, but she wanted so much more which he wasn't prepared to give.

'You wanted me to last night.'

'Last night was different.' Couldn't he see that? Evidently he couldn't. 'You were able to forget that I was out of your class,' he reminded her.

She shook her head impatiently. 'Yes, but I can't forget that I'm out of yours.'

His eyes darkened with confusion. 'You aren't making sense. How could you be out of my class?'

'Easily. You're everything I dream of being—strong, independent. You know what you want from your life and how to get it.' Her voice tailed away on a sigh of despair.

'Surely you could be all those things if you wanted to?'

She chewed her lower lip thoughtfully. 'It isn't so easy after a lifetime of being conditioned to conform.'

His look of puzzlement turned to anger as he released her and walked away. 'Well, it's nice to know I've been part of your emancipation.'

His derisive tone sliced through her like a knife. 'You're determined to see me in the worst light, aren't you?' she demanded. Tears clustered at the backs of her eyes, and she blinked furiously. He wasn't going to make her cry, damn him. 'Can't you see, you're equally guilty of snobbery?'

He swung around, his lip curling into a sneer. 'Well, at least it's more honest than your kind of snobbery.'

With hands on her hips and legs wide apart, she faced him like a cornered animal, a wild creature fighting for survival. 'Is it? I'm here, aren't I? I slept on a rug on the floor of your cabin, wrapped in a blanket. What's snobbish about that?'

He stared at her in astonishment, the anger in his eyes turned amazingly to respect. Then she was stunned to hear him laugh, the sound rich and rolling, reaching out to her in a caress of sound. 'You have a point,' he conceded when his laughter stopped. 'Your behaviour was as unspoiled as could be, except for one thing.'

'What's that?' she asked, intrigued.

'You were right about sleeping on the floor in a blanket, but you did it wearing a Cartier watch.'

Her glance flew to her wrist. She had forgotten she was wearing the watch, a birthday present from her father. She had indeed spent the night on a rug in a wilderness cabin, naked except for her diamond-studded watch.

Their shared laughter dispelled some of the tension. When she started making breakfast, the atmosphere was degrees warmer than before. She was glad Dane had noticed the watch and made a joke out of it.

But, even as she cracked the eggs for their breakfast omelette, the watch winked up at her accusingly. To her it was just a watch, treasured because it was a gift from her father. But to many people it was a status symbol, and to Dane it was a symbol of all that stood between them.

CHAPTER SIX

IT WAS mid-morning by the time they finished the chores, partly because the cabin possessed none of the labour-saving gadgets which Evelyn was used to, and partly because Dane felt moved to kiss her every so often.

'It's a shame you have to go back to your own cabin,' he said.

'You know why I have to. Dad's a stickler for detail, and he won't consider I'm keeping my end of our bet if I share your quarters.'

He lifted one ash-coloured eyebrow. 'Does he have to know?'

'You're not suggesting I cheat?'

He shrugged. 'Maybe you have already.'

She looked at him in dismay. 'You don't think I've already blown it by spending the night here, do you?'

He rescued the tea-towel she was in danger of shredding, and began to dry their breakfast dishes. 'As I understand it, the deal is that you spend a month looking after yourself. That means doing your own cooking and chores, right? Well that's what you're doing right now.'

She chewed her lower lip thoughtfully. 'I hope you're right.'

'And there's always the wood-chopping,' he reminded her, with a gleam in his eyes. 'Or do I have to motivate you for that?'

She had no doubt what sort of motivation he had in mind. 'No, thank you,' she said primly. 'Besides, you chopped enough to last for days.'

He hung the tea-towel over a chair to dry. 'Pity. Then we'd better head down to the jetty and meet Ned's boat.'

'Ned's boat? But I thought he only called once a fortnight.'

'If you check your calendar, you'll find that's today.'

Her eyes widened with astonishment. 'Have I been here for two weeks already? The time has gone so quickly.'

'It's exactly two weeks since you arrived. We should have a celebration in honour of the occasion.'

'What would you suggest?'

He grinned. 'I know what I'd like to suggest, but I think I'll have to settle for a beach picnic. Remember I promised to show you the Friar's Cave.'

'I'd love to see it,' she enthused. 'Is it far?'

'On the other side of the island, where I keep my boat. So wear your comfy walking-shoes.'

'I will. And I'll bring the picnic.'

'You're on. We'll set off as soon as we've unloaded your supplies and stowed them away.'

When he added the last part, she smiled, remembering what had happened to the first lot of supplies she'd left unattended on the jetty. This time, they weren't taking any chances.

They arrived at the timber jetty in time to see Ned's thirty-foot cruiser appear on the horizon. Evelyn glimpsed the crusty old seafarer on the flying bridge.

She noticed the figures moving around the deck of the cruiser. 'He has some other people with him; I wonder who they are.'

'Day-trippers, most likely.'

She recalled Ned telling her that he took parties of tourists cruising around these waters. She hoped they didn't plan to stop at Frere Island. She was looking forward to spending the day alone with Dane, exploring Friar's Cave.

But, as soon as the cruiser pulled in at the little jetty, she knew they would have to revise their plans. Her heart sank as she recognised Ned's passengers.

'Julie and Jerry, what a surprise!' she called weakly as Ned tied his boat up.

Julie Cummings jumped nimbly ashore, ignoring Ned's offered hand. 'Hi, Evelyn. My darling brother was determined not to celebrate his birthday without you, so we brought the party to you.'

Evelyn felt her knees weaken. 'You what?'

'Oh, not the whole gang. Just Jerry, me and the Mutt.'

'You didn't bring your dog?'

Jerry jumped down beside them, dusting off his designer jeans. 'I don't go anywhere without the Mutt, you know that.'

Sure enough, a third passenger emerged from the cabin, a large, hairy animal which Evelyn recognised as Jerry's dog, Mutt. A cross between a labrador and a setter, he was lovable enough, but he was also the most undisciplined dog Evelyn had ever known.

For a moment, politeness warred with the urge to send them back to the mainland, dog and all. Breeding won. 'Hello, Jerry, good to see you,' she said, extending a limp hand.

Jerry and Julie Cummings were friends from Evelyn's schooldays. Julie took Evelyn's hand and leaned across the dog's bulk to kiss her cheek. 'Aren't you thrilled to have some company?'

Despite her careful upbringing, Evelyn was sorely tempted to be honest. 'You're welcome,' she said, hating herself for the lie. 'Did you come for the day?'

Julie laughed. 'No, silly. We came to stay the night. Ned is coming back to pick us up tomorrow morning.'

'But I don't have enough beds or anything. And I'm sure there isn't enough food.'

'Yes, there is, we brought our own supplies.' Jerry hefted a Gucci cabin-bag and it clanked alarmingly. It sounded as if most of Jerry's supplies were of the liquid kind. She had a suspicion he had been working on them already.

She gave Ned a helpless look. 'I wish I'd known you were bringing guests.'

He shrugged, but his expression was sympathetic. 'I tried to let you know, but I couldn't reach you on the phone last night and they insisted on coming with me today. Your phone must have been playing up.'

'Maybe it wasn't the phone. Maybe Evelyn was playing up,' Jerry interjected, digging her in the side with his elbow. 'Did you find something interesting to do on your lonely little island? A Man Friday or a Man Monday-to-Saturday, perhaps?'

'Cut it out, Jerry,' his sister instructed.

Evelyn gave her a wan smile. 'It's all right, Julie. I suppose we should blame the high spirits on his birthday.'

'It was two days ago and he's still celebrating,' Julie said, an edge of tiredness in her voice. 'But I admit, I was curious to see what you'd got yourself into. You missed all the summer parades. I bought this divine cocktail dress for the Christmas season. You should see it. It's...'

'Tell me later,' Evelyn cut in, trying not to sound as edgy as she felt. It wasn't the first time that Julie had discussed her clothes purchases with Evelyn, stitch by stitch, and she was usually attentive. But there was something incongruous about discussing the latest fashions on the jetty of an unspoilt island.

She turned to Ned, who had nearly finished unloading her supplies. 'I'll take them up from here, thanks.'

He nodded. 'You'll have plenty of help this time, at least.'

She wasn't counting on it where these two were concerned, but she could depend on Dane, who had already promised to give her a hand.

But when she swung around to look for him he had vanished. She had been so sidetracked by the arrival of her friends that she hadn't noticed him leave. 'Lost something?' Jerry asked, seeing her look around.

Now wasn't the time to tell them about the man who was sharing the island. 'No, nothing,' she said, and bent to pick up one of the boxes.

As she'd expected, the others weren't much help, but they saved her a couple of trips. Jerry, she noticed, picked up the smallest and lightest load and became very busy adjusting his Reeboks when it was time to go back for more. 'Join you as soon as I get this stone out of my shoe,' he said, waving her past.

'Stay here, I'll manage,' she said resignedly. On the way back to the jetty, she wondered if she had seemed as useless to Dane as Jerry looked to her now. No wonder he hadn't had much time for her.

Where had he gone? she wondered. He must have seen that she had all the help she needed and decided not to stick around. But he could have waited long enough for her to introduce him to her friends, she thought irritably.

He might not want an introduction, she acknowledged reluctantly. He had already warned her that he wanted no part of her world. That included her friends, she supposed.

By the time she'd brought the last box up from the jetty, Jerry was sprawled on a folding lounger outside the cabin. Mutt lay like a discarded fur coat at his feet. The sound of a heavy metal band emanating from his portable disc player shattered the island peace. Birds screeched in alarm at the alien sounds.

'Turn it down, Jerry,' she begged, shouting to be heard over the throbbing music.

'What?'

She pantomimed her request and he reached for the player's controls. The throbbing subsided a little and she muttered her thanks. Mutt's tail thumped feebly in appreciation.

Jerry looked perplexed. 'I thought you'd enjoy something a bit more upbeat after hearing nothing but the birds and the bees for two weeks.'

'I happen to like the birds and the bees. I didn't even miss radio or television.' Until now, she hadn't even thought about the lack. The island possessed too many other benefits. Like Dane Balkan, she thought wistfully. Much as she liked Julie Cummings, and tolerated Jerry for Julie's sake, she wished they hadn't come.

Julie emerged from the cabin carrying tall glasses of iced liquid. 'I thought you'd be ready for this by now. I raided your fridge. It's only cordial, but you don't seem to have anything stronger in stock.'

'A trifle, soon mended,' Jerry said airily. He reached into the Gucci bag alongside his chair and pulled out a flask of dark liquid. 'Rum. Goes with most cordials,' he explained. He poured a generous splash into his glass, then offered the flask to Evelyn.

She shuddered and shook her head. 'No, thanks. I hate the taste of rum.' In truth, she disliked most strong spirits, and drank them well diluted with soft drinks, usually to be sociable. Here she had no one to impress, no need to pretend.

'Hey, dreamer, I asked you a question.'

She jerked her attention back to the others. 'Sorry. What did you say?'

Julie grinned. 'Two weeks alone on an island is getting to you. We arrived just in the nick of time, didn't we, Jerry?'

He took a long pull on his drink. 'So it seems. Except that Evelyn hasn't been alone, have you, darling?'

She felt the colour begin to creep up her face and bent her head over her cordial. 'I don't know what you mean.'

'Oh, no? What about that unshaven hunk who was standing on the jetty beside you this morning?'

Damn! Since neither of her friends had mentioned Dane, she had convinced herself they had missed seeing him. She should have known it wouldn't be that simple. 'He's—um—he's staying in a cabin on the other side of the island.'

Julie's brows knitted in concentration. 'I thought this was your island.'

'It is. I didn't know he was staying here until the day I arrived. His lease is valid for six months, so I can't do anything about him.'

A teasing grin tugged at the corners of Julie's mouth. 'Why on earth would you want to, if he's—what did Jerry call him—a hunk?'

In spite of herself, Evelyn was provoked. 'He's not a hunk or unshaven. He's a scientist, here to work on a research project.'

Jerry snorted derisively. 'Some scientist. He could give Tom Selleck a run for his money. I'm sure I know him from somewhere.'

'You must introduce me to this scientist,' Julie put in. 'Maybe we could do some research together. I could think of a few subjects he'd find interesting.'

'Forget it, he's practically a hermit,' Evelyn insisted. 'He came with me this morning to help with the supplies, that's all.'

'Methinks she doth protest too much,' Jerry intoned. He reached down and ruffled Mutt's thick fur. 'What do you think, boy? Is our Evelyn besotted, or what?'

Evelyn jumped to her feet. Her feelings for Dane were too volatile to bear Jerry's unsubtle teasing. Her only defence was to pretend indifference to Dane. 'You've got to be joking. How could I fall for a drop-out like him? You said yourself he's unshaven. I don't think he's noticed I'm female yet.'

'Poor guy. He must be loony as well as unsociable. I knew you were female as soon as I set eyes on that gorgeous body of yours.' Uncoiling himself from the lounger, Jerry came up behind her and twined his fingers in her hair. She could feel his hot breath on the back of her neck, and the smell of rum on it made her feel nauseous.

She moved away. 'Not everybody has your taste, Jerry.'

He sighed theatrically. 'How true. But if it means the mad scientist hasn't stolen a march on me yet, I have to be grateful.'

Jerry's callous description of Dane made her blood boil, but she knew that reacting to it would only make him tease her more cruelly, so she bit back a reply. But there was one thing she couldn't let pass. 'I wasn't aware there was any march to steal,' she said carefully.

His eyes narrowed. 'It's always been you and me. Kismet and all that,' he said. 'Besides, I have your father's blessing.'

She was tempted to suggest that he should marry her father, in that case, but held her tongue. Jerry was a fool, but dangerous if provoked, and she had already given him too much ammunition. 'Why don't we go for a swim?' she suggested to break the tension.

'Good idea,' Julie said heartily. 'It will be a change from listening to you two having a lover's tiff.'

Even Julie regarded them as a couple, Evelyn thought with a sinking heart. She would have to make sure that Jerry understood her true feelings before he left. She would hate him to spread the news all over the mainland that they were a couple. It wasn't true, and never would be.

The glorious weather reminded her of when she had first arrived, she thought as she led the way down the bush path towards the swimming-hole. They had debated the merits of swimming in the ocean versus the lagoon at the centre of the island, and had opted for the quiet inland waters.

A native currawong flapped across her path and the scent of wild flowers invaded her nostrils. If only she were going to meet Dane at the pool.

But she wasn't, and the persistent beat of music from Jerry's portable player was a constant reminder. The sound was almost obscene in such a paradise, like a snake in the garden of Eden. As if the music wasn't enough, Jerry's penetrating voice followed her as he commented unfavourably on everything.

The path wasn't wide enough. She should have it cleared and paved. The trees should be pruned back so that they didn't catch at one's face. The birds were too noisy, although how he could hear them over the racket of his player she didn't know. Finally she'd had enough.

'Why did you bother coming if you dislike roughing it?' she demanded, her eyes blazing at him as she looked back over her shoulder.

'Just what I've been asking myself,' he said sulkily. Then his gaze wandered over her, stopping at her bikini-clad behind. 'On the other hand, there are compensations.'

The crocheted two-piece was the only swimsuit she had brought. When she'd suggested a swim, she had forgotten that it would mean exposing herself in her brief suit. Jerry's interest confirmed her worst fears. It was just as well that his sister was with them as chaperon.

She looked back to see Julie dropping behind, hindered by the dog she was trying to control. Evelyn had insisted that if Mutt came along it was on a leash. The animal was clearly unhappy with the arrangement.

So was Jerry. 'It's inhuman to treat Mutt like that.'

'He wouldn't strain so if you'd taught him properly,' Evelyn reminded him. 'He'll get used to it.'

'No, he won't. He's suffering because of your Tarzan's rat population. It isn't fair.'

She bristled. 'He isn't Tarzan. His name is Dane. And they're not rats, they are Tasmanian Devils.'

He shrugged. 'A rat by any other name... and speaking of names, I've heard that one somewhere.'

'Tasmanian Devil?' she asked innocently.

'No, Dane. What's the rest of it?'

'It doesn't matter, we're here,' she said, relief in her voice. They emerged at the foot of the miniature waterfall which fed the freshwater lagoon where she had first seen Dane swimming.

She looked upwards, spotting the tangle of vegetation where she had slid down the hillside to his feet. Quickly she averted her gaze.

Then she was drawn back to the spot as a movement in the bushes caught her eye. Dane was up there, watching them. The discovery made her bristle with annoyance. Why couldn't he come down and meet her friends, like a civilised person? Because he wasn't civilised, she decided. He didn't care for the conventions. Yet, without them, where would people be? If everyone did their own thing, as he chose to do, society would be in chaos.

She was being defensive, she realised. He had made her see her friends, and herself, in a light she didn't care for. The music, the drinking, even Jerry's complaints, wouldn't have bothered her once, if she'd noticed them at all. Dane had made her see things differently, then abandoned her. She hated him for that.

'Last one in's a rotten so-and-so,' Jerry called out. He had shed his possessions on a flat rock overlooking the pool, and took a running jump off

the ledge. There was a mighty splash as he landed
and Evelyn was showered with water.

'Fool,' she muttered. She was about to jump in
herself, but couldn't resist another look upwards.
Dane was still there, leaning against a Huon pine,
his body screened from the others by a clump of
Man ferns. She had the strangest feeling that he
was laughing at her.

Well, she would show him. 'Coming, ready or
not,' she called loudly enough for Dane to hear,
then jumped into the water.

It was icy and she came up spluttering. Jerry was
beside her and he scooped her up in his arms. 'Fear
not, fair maid. I've got you.'

Her anger at Dane was still fresh in her mind.
Instead of pushing Jerry away, she clasped her arms
around his neck. 'Thank you for saving me, Jerry
dear.'

'My privilege, fair lady. But you didn't ask me
what I was saving you for.'

She tossed her head back, managing to look as
if she was laughing at Jerry, while she scanned the
treeline above them. She was in time to see Dane
turn and disappear into the bushes.

Disgusted with herself, she pushed free of Jerry's
arms and struck out for the shore. He stood in the
chest-high water, looking after her in puzzlement,
then dived under the waterfall and came up on the
far side, swimming strongly. Clinging to a rock at
the water's edge, she watched him swim laps of the
small pool, his anger showing in the jerky thrusts
of his arms and legs.

'What's the matter with him?' Julie asked, surfacing beside her and sweeping damp strands of hair off her forehead.

'Me, I think,' Evelyn said glumly. 'It would be so simple if I felt the way he does.'

'Don't worry about it,' Julie said, surprising her. 'Jerry doesn't feel anything, for you or anybody. Everything bores him and he has to go after bigger and better stimulation just to feel anything at all.'

Evelyn regarded her friend in amazement. 'I thought you wanted us to get together.'

Julie's beautiful mouth pursed elegantly. 'It was wishful thinking, I suppose. You'd be good for him, but I can see that he wouldn't be good for you. I'm sorry we broke in on your holiday.'

Lying back in the cool water, Evelyn sighed. 'It isn't your fault. I'm just not very good company right now.'

'Is it the man in the other cottage?'

'Why does it have to be a man?'

'It doesn't, but you were so defensive about him this morning. Then you acted as if you didn't give a hoot. I think Jerry was right. You are protesting too much.'

Overhead, the sky seemed unbelievably perfect and distant, like her feelings for Dane. 'You're right,' she acknowledged. 'But it doesn't matter, because he is a drop-out. I wasn't making that up. He has no time for me or my life-style.'

'Which explains why he didn't stay around to be introduced. What rotten luck to fall in love with a primitive who thinks money is a curse.'

Julie was right, she knew. Only it wasn't the money which Dane despised. It was the life-style it engendered, selfish and demanding, the way she herself had been in danger of becoming until she came to the island. But it was too late. Dane had made up his mind about her, and not even what they'd shared last night was going to change it.

One good thing came out of the scene at the pool, she discovered that evening. Jerry made no more attempts to force his attention on to her. She wondered if Julie had said something to him, but kept the thought to herself.

He was drinking steadily, she noticed with concern. He had hardly eaten anything of the chicken casserole she'd concocted for dinner, and spent the evening staring morosely into his glass.

'Hardly the life of the party,' Julie observed, glancing at him.

'At least he can't drive anywhere. There are no cars on the island.'

They looked up in concern as Jerry lurched to his feet. 'I'm going to take Mutt for a walk,' he announced.

'I'll do it,' Julie volunteered.

He waved an arm at her. 'No problem. I'd like to do some thinking, anyway. C'mon, Mutt.' He whistled to the dog, which jumped up, wagging its tail expectantly at the word 'walk'. The two of them went out together.

'Will he be all right, do you think?' Julie asked anxiously.

Evelyn hastened to reassure her. 'He's walking steadily enough. I don't think he's as drunk as he wanted us to think. Maybe it's an excuse to avoid talking to us.'

Julie regarded her with respect. 'You're smarter than you look. Even if you did fall for Tarzan by mistake.'

Evelyn drew a pattern on the table with a forefinger. 'I'd rather not talk about him if you don't mind. Tell me all about the spring parades and your new dress.'

It was the right thing to say, because Julie promptly launched into an enthusiastic account of the new season's fashions. Evelyn let her thoughts drift, distantly aware of Julie's description of her new dress. It all seemed so far away and unimportant, somehow.

Her reverie was interrupted by a furious barking sound outside, following by a cacophony of spitting and snarling noises. Julie looked at her in alarm. 'What's that?'

'Where did Jerry go, do you know?' she asked her friend urgently.

Julie looked blank. 'He said earlier he saw some funny possums Mutt might like to chase.'

'They're not possums. They're Dane's Tasmanian Devils.'

Julie's concern subsided. 'That's all right, then. They can hold their own against a dog, can't they?'

'No, that's a myth. They only look fierce, but a dog can easily kill one.' She jumped to her feet. 'I'm going to find them.'

Locating Jerry and Mutt was simply a matter of following the dreadful noise to its source. She found Jerry sheltering behind a tree while Mutt, his leash

trailing, jumped and barked, trying to reach something on a low branch over his head. Evelyn recognised the spitting, snarling creature at once.

She tugged at Jerry's arm. 'That's Henrietta.
You've got to call Mutt off before he hurts her.'

He laughed. 'Why should I? He's only behaving
like a dog.'

He wasn't the only one, she thought savagely.
She smelled a pungent odour in the air and on
Jerry's clothes. 'You've been smoking something.'

His laughter became more hysterical. 'What if I
have? There are no cops around here. Who's going
to stop me?'

'I am.'

Dane erupted into the clearing like an avenging
spirit, his tall, lean form stalking them with deadly
purpose. With a sweep of one powerful arm, he
sent Jerry sprawling, then he advanced on the animals. 'Get down!' he ordered in a thunderous voice.

Mutt's frenzied barking trailed off into a whine
and he backed away from Dane, sensing a threat.
'Go on,' he said in the same unrelenting tone. The
dog slunk around the edge of the clearing to Jerry,
who sat on the ground looking stunned. He clasped
an arm around the dog's mane.

'OK, Henrietta. Everything's OK.'

Evelyn stared in astonishment, hearing Dane's
voice change to a gentle murmur which soothed the
Tasmanian Devil. Henrietta's ruffled fur settled
down and the spitting and snarling stopped. She
stayed on the tree trunk, her long claws digging into
the wood, but she didn't resist when Dane lifted
her down from the tree and set her on the ground.

'Go on, off you go,' he urged. Without a backward look, the Tasmanian Devil ran off into the underbrush.

Catching sight of Dane's grim expression as he whirled on her made Evelyn wish she could do the same. Jerry had taken advantage of the moment to head back to the cabin, tugging Mutt with him on the leash. She and Dane were alone.

'Will Henrietta be all right?' she asked, hearing her voice come out shaky.

'Probably, no thanks to you and your friend,' he said curtly. 'Or is it lover?'

'Either way, it's none of your business,' she snapped back. Hurt made her want to lash out at him and make him suffer as she was suffering. She'd tried to save Henrietta from the dog. Couldn't Dane give her any credit for that?

It seemed not. 'You're quite right, it is none of my business, and I couldn't give a damn who else you sleep with.' He put such cruel emphasis on the word *else* that she felt as if he had stung her with a lash instead of just his tongue. She flinched away from him, but he didn't seem to notice. 'You did warn me that I wasn't the only one,' he went on. 'At least you saved me from a guilty conscience.'

Would he have had a conscience about making love to her then abandoning her? she wondered bleakly. It was more than she'd expected. 'You're wrong about there being others,' she said bleakly, tears stinging her eyes. 'There was a man, once. I loved him and wanted to marry him, but my father sent him away.'

'Am I supposed to believe you after the touching scene I witnessed between you and Jerry this afternoon?'

'I knew you were there. I wanted to get even, so I played up to him,' she defended herself.

His sensuous mouth tightened into a sneer. 'Which proves my case. You have no compunction about using people.'

What could she say? She was damned out of her own mouth. 'All the same, you're wrong,' she insisted.

He gestured dismissively. 'It doesn't matter now. But you can tell your friends that if they or their dog ever trouble these animals again, I won't answer for my actions. Is that clear?'

The irony of his threat, when it was she who owned the island, didn't take away the sting of his words. 'I'll tell them,' she said dully.

He swung around and she heard him striding off down the bush path in the direction of his cabin. The animals would be gathering for their evening meal, she thought, recalling the joy of sharing the moment. Now she never would again. No matter how many months she spent on the island, they would be worlds apart from now on.

With a heavy heart she trudged back to her own cabin. Mutt, still excited, ran to meet her at the door. She patted him absently, unable to blame him for the havoc tonight. But she could and did blame Jerry, although he looked so miserable that she bit back her words of condemnation.

Julie was sitting beside him, and they had been deep in conversation which her arrival had interrupted. 'Are you all right?' Julie asked her.

'I'm fine,' she said automatically. She was halfway up the stairs to her loft when Jerry's words stopped her.

'You know, I've just remembered where I've seen your Dane before.'

CHAPTER SEVEN

A CHILL of foreboding crept down Evelyn's back and a shiver rippled through her. Gripping the rickety railing with a white-knuckled hand, she looked down at Jerry. He no longer acted penitent. His shoulders were straight and his eyes blazed. He would never forgive Dane for humiliating him tonight. She couldn't trust anything he told her.

Still, it took every ounce of will-power to remain on the stairs and say with studied insouciance, 'Tell me in the morning.'

Watched by his sister, a worried frown on her face, he came to the foot of the stairs. 'OK. But at least I understand now why you prefer him to me.'

'That's ridiculous.' The denial was automatic, and sounded false even to her own ears.

'Is it? When Tarzan stormed on to the scene outside, your expression was a dead giveaway. If I didn't know he was loaded, I'd be jealous as hell. Come to think of it, I am jealous as hell, but I can't compete with Balkan's fortune.'

It was all she could do not to clap both hands over her ears like a child, to shut out the unwelcome sound of Jerry's voice. She didn't want to respond. His claims were absurd, both about her feelings and about Dane being wealthy. 'You're wrong,' she said, unable to stop herself in the end.

112

A triumphant grin spread over Jerry's face, and she could have kicked herself for taking his bait. 'What did *you* get wrong, your feelings? Because it isn't his background,' he said. 'He's changed his appearance a lot since he went loopy. I'm more used to seeing him in a three-piece suit on the floor of the Stock Exchange.'

Relief made her knees go weak and she sat down on the middle step. 'I already know he was a broker in Hobart. It's no big secret. But he gave it up. He's broke now. His ex-wife got most of his money when they split up.'

Jerry laughed, the sound reminding her of a fingernail drawn across a blackboard. 'Is that what he told you? I wish I'd known you were a sucker for a hard-luck story, I'd have tried it myself. Not that you'd have believed me.'

It was too late to stop now. 'You may as well tell me the rest,' she said on a sigh of resignation.

'I don't know, what's it worth?'

'Jerry, for pity's sake, can't you see this is important to Evelyn?' Julie cut in.

Evelyn gave her a grateful glance. Jerry's look was not so appreciative, but he draped himself over the railing. 'Very well, since you're obviously in good and deep. Balkan came from nowhere, a farm boy, I think they said he was. He went to the same school as I did, but on a scholarship. He was a couple of years ahead of me so I didn't really know him, but he was supposed to be a maths whiz, a genius. A few years ago, he predicted a gold boom and bought enough futures to make a killing when the price finally rose.'

It was an effort to contain her impatience. 'Lots of people made money in gold then. Dad was among them.'

'So who do you think advised him to? Balkan practically doubled your father's fortune overnight. It was in all the financial pages, but I don't suppose you read those.'

Numbly, she shook her head. 'Dad never discusses business at home,' she added, thinking that he never discussed business with her any time, anywhere. How else could she be so blind to Dane's background?

'So you really didn't know? Poor kid. You'd think your father would have entertained Balkan at home, considering he made a lot of your lifestyle possible.'

Her father was vain about his image as a self-made man, at least to his family. She couldn't imagine him inviting Dane to his home. Generally, his employees were well paid, while he reserved any credit for his success for himself. She felt slightly sick. 'Dane could still be telling the truth about losing his money,' she persisted.

'I wouldn't know about that,' Jerry said. 'There wasn't a whisper about the divorce in the papers. I only knew through a friend of his wife's. A condition of the settlement was that she didn't make it public. But I do know that Balkan is still a director of several companies and a majority shareholder in one of the country's largest gold-mines. They're still producing, so it's hard to see how he can be on his uppers. My guess is he has more money than you and me put together. But don't take my word for it. Why don't you ask your father?'

'I intend to.'

The savage way she spoke made Jerry regard her anxiously. 'I hope I'm not talking out of turn.'

'Is there any other way for you to talk?' They both looked surprised as Julie joined them at the foot of the stairs. In her distress, Evelyn had forgotten she was listening to all that was said. Now she touched Evelyn's arm in a gesture of concern. 'Are you all right?'

Holding on to her composure with every ounce of will-power she possessed, Evelyn nodded. 'Of course, I'm fine.'

Still, Julie wasn't deceived. 'If Dane told you he was broke, he must have had a reason.'

She stood up. 'I'm sure he did,' she agreed, then finished her climb to the loft, her head high.

Yes, he had a reason, she felt certain. His put-down of her wealth and social position was a cover, designed to disguise his real purpose here. For she had no doubt that he had been planted by her father, with the express purpose of sabotaging her attempt at independence.

Oddly enough, she was angrier with her father than with Dane. In her experience, businessmen stuck together. The more rich and powerful they were, the more loyal they were to each other. The proof of it was in her father's attitude to her brother, Alex. He was automatically part of their exclusive club. As a woman, she was forever excluded.

Dane belonged to their club. He would be the ideal person for her father to send here. The tragedy was, the ploy had worked beyond her father's wildest dreams.

For Jerry was right, she had fallen in love with Dane. Believing him to be everything she wanted to be, she had given him her whole heart and more. The thought of how much more made her choke with misery. How he must have laughed the night she'd gone into his arms, like a lamb to the slaughter. She had been afraid he would think she did it all the time, when he was the one who should have apologised to her. It galled her to think how easily she had played into his hands.

And he had the nerve to accuse her of using people!

Although it was late, she knew she wouldn't sleep until she had spoken to her father. Maybe it wasn't too late for him to recall Dane and go on with their original deal.

The thought that Dane might tell her father that they had spent the night together sickened her, even though she found it hard to believe that he would stoop so low. Her father would almost certainly use it against her. Knowing how Dane had already lied to her didn't give her much confidence in his discretion.

Around her, the cottage grew quiet. After she had come to bed, she had heard Julie and Jerry talking, then everything went quiet. They were probably asleep on the banquettes she had turned into beds for them in the living-room. If she was quiet, she could make her call from the kitchen without disturbing them.

The cabin seemed to hold its breath as she tiptoed down the stairs again, drawing in her breath at each creak of the rickety stairs. Outside, a wind had sprung up, turning the stillness into a rustling, crackling nightmare. A tree branch scraped across the cabin roof, the sound eerily like someone shuffling along in carpet slippers. She shook herself mentally. She was on edge. There was nothing outside but the bush with its friendly creatures— and Dane. She stifled a sob.

Despite the late hour, her father could still be in his office, so she tried that number first. Instead of a ringing tone, there was a high-pitched whine. She frowned at it and tried her home number, getting the same response. Ned must be right, the phone was out of order. Guiltily, she had assumed he'd been unable to get through because she'd been staying with Dane. It hadn't occurred to her that the line was out of order. She hadn't thought to check it during the day. Now she had no means of contacting her father. Frustration gnawed at her.

Next morning, after tossing and turning for most of the night, she reached a decision. She couldn't ask her father about Dane's presence here, so she would have to ask Dane himself. It might be less painful to hear the truth from her father, but she doubted it. The ache inside her was already more than she could bear. Nothing could make it worse.

Julie and Jerry were still rolled up in their blankets when she let herself out of the cottage. It had rained during the night, the roof leaking again but not too badly. Now the island steamed gently in the morning sun. The air was fragrant with herbal scents as she crushed the moist plants underfoot, but she was in no mood to appreciate the beauty of the new day.

As she had expected, Dane was already up and about. He looked up in surprise when she burst into the clearing, scattering a family of rosellas who were feeding on a clump of fluffy yellow wattle. 'I want to talk to you.'

'If it's about last night, I make no apology for the way I acted. Your friend Jerry is the one you should give your lecture to.'

'I didn't come for an apology. I don't blame you for being angry about the Tasmanian Devils. I was angry, too.'

His gaze softened as the pale eyes rested on her. She had dressed carelessly in a Jenny Kee silk shirt and tight-fitting Levi jeans. The shirt draped over her breasts, falling open at the cleft. When Dane's gaze went to it and the muscles in his jaw began to work, it was an effort not to clutch the shirt-front closed. She didn't want to turn him on right now. Nor did she welcome the warmth which flooded through her at the sight of his sculptured torso which gleamed as if he'd been anointed with oil. As usual he was shirtless, his jeans riding low on narrow hips. Her pulses jumped and she licked her lips nervously.

It was some consolation that he seemed equally disturbed by her presence. 'If it wasn't about last night, why did you come?'

She was tempted to say she couldn't stay away, just to see how he reacted. But because it was so nearly true she swallowed the words. 'I came for the truth,' she said instead. 'Why didn't you tell me you were my father's broker?'

She waited for him to deny it, unconsciously hoping he would, she realised. Instead, he shrugged carelessly, the muscles swelling at the movement. 'In the first place, you didn't ask. And in the second, I'm not "his" broker. He was one of my clients, that's all. Is it important?'

'To me, it is. Do all your clients get you to do their dirty work?'

His eyes darkened with anger. 'What the hell does that mean?'

'It means I know he sent you here to prevent me from winning my bet.'

'You think a lot of yourself if you imagine I have nothing better to do than play nursemaid to a spoiled brat of an heiress.'

She folded her arms across her chest. 'The name-calling would be effective if I didn't know you're worth as much as I am, if not more.'

He half closed his eyes. The hooded look reminded her of an eagle, measuring up its prey. 'So Jerry's been telling tales, has he?'

'He only told me the truth, which is more than you saw fit to do.'

He threw down the armload of firewood he'd been carrying, and dusted the timber chips off his hands. She waited in silence, watching him.

At last he approached her, hands extended. 'I didn't mention my connection with your father because I knew you'd be unreasonable about it.'

'Is it unreasonable to object to being spied on and compromised?'

His laughter exploded on the still morning air. 'Compromised? You sound like something out of a comedy of manners. If you mean I made love to you, why not say so?'

Embarrassed by his frankness, she plucked a wand of wattle blossom and played with it to avoid having to meet his eyes. 'All right, we made love. What I want to know is why.'

'I thought we both wanted to.'

This time she raised her head, but his eyes remained hooded and unreadable. 'I wanted it. I thought you felt the same way.'

'So what made you decide I didn't?'

Golden powder showered to the ground as she shredded the wattle spray in nerveless fingers. 'I know you didn't. If you really cared for me, you wouldn't have lied about everything.'

He closed the small remaining gap between them, and she sucked in a sharp breath as he grasped her shoulders. There was no way to avoid looking at him. 'When did I lie?' he demanded. His tone was soft but steely. 'Tell me. I want to know.'

The fiery brand of his touch seared her through her shirt. It was a reminder of other moments and other touches which were gentle and caressing. Had she moved but slightly, his hands would have slid around her back and she could have rested her head against the reassuring bulk of his shoulder. He had showered recently. The spicy scent of soap still clung to him. Unsteadily, she breathed in.

'I'm waiting,' he repeated softly.

She steadied her breathing and willed herself not to weaken. 'You told me Janice took all your money,' she said. 'Then you pretended your ideals made you different from me.'

His breath whistled out softly. 'That's quite an indictment, but it doesn't prove I lied to you.'

'But you said...'

'I hadn't finished,' he cut in, silencing her. 'I'm entitled to answer the charges.' She nodded dumbly. 'First, Janice did take all my money—all I had at the time of our divorce. I told you I could make more. I have no intention of being poor. You chose to interpret what I said your own way. Correct?'

Now she thought about it, she could see how she might have reached the wrong conclusion. She had wanted to believe that he was different from the men she knew. 'Yes,' she said reluctantly.

He nodded as if satisfied. 'As to the second charge, my ideals do make me different. That's no lie. I did come here to re-evaluate my life. After Janice left, I decided there was more to life than chasing the next dollar so that someone else could spend it for me.'

The truth of his statements seemed undeniable. She moved restlessly under the imprisoning weight of his grasp. 'I'm sorry if I misjudged you,' she said in a voice barely above a whisper.

His gaze mellowed. 'You saw what you wanted to see in me. I warned you against it.'

There was a tree trunk at her back. She leaned against it as if for protection. 'I know, but it doesn't change the way I feel.'

'It should.'

'I know.'

His voice dropped to a husky whisper. Hers deepened in response. The fighting spirit drained out of her as she met his warm gaze. This time she felt no need to cover her breasts. Contrarily, she was proud of her ability to arouse him, to make him want her, even when he had just explained why it wouldn't work.

She watched him war with himself, then surrender with a harsh outrush of breath. When he kissed her, it was with a fierce urgency which sent shafts of longing all the way to the core of her being.

The last of her anger died as he shaped her mouth to his and parted her lips with his tongue, to plunge hungrily inside. As far as she was concerned, there was no part of her that didn't welcome his touch. She craved it. She needed it. He could insist that they were better off apart, but he couldn't make her believe it.

His kiss wandered from her mouth across her jawline and down the column of her throat. Breathing became a struggle. Of their own accord, her hands splayed across his sun-warmed back, and she explored every ridge of his muscular torso with eager fingers.

She offered no resistance when he nuzzled aside the silk of her shirt and slid his tongue down the inviting cleft he laid bare. The sensation was unbelievable, and shudders of pure pleasure rocked her.

He felt the response and held her more tightly in the circle of his arms. She reacted by sliding her fingers along the waistband of his jeans, her fingertips dipping teasingly inside. When she worked her way around to the fastening and began to free it, he gave a groan of defeat and pulled her hard against him. 'You came to make war, not love,' he reminded her hoarsely.

Her throat ached, but she summoned her voice. 'Can't I change my mind?'

'Woman's prerogative,' he murmured, his lips against her hairline. 'The hell with war. I'd much rather make love.'

His arm was warm around her waist as he started to lead her into his cabin. The thought of the fur rug waiting by the fireside sent a thrill of anticipation through her.

Dreamily she leaned her head against his shoulder. 'I'm so glad you have nothing to do with my father,' she murmured.

At once she felt his tension increase. His footsteps slowed. 'I didn't say that,' he corrected her.

An icy coolness overtook her as she realised he hadn't denied that part of her charge. Lifting her head, she stepped out of the circle of his arms. 'What are you saying—that you *did* come here on Dad's behalf?'

'Nothing of the sort. I only agreed to keep an eye on you for him.'

'So you are working for him?'

He reached for her but she shook off his hand. 'Be reasonable, Evelyn. You're the daughter of an important man. He was worried about you. He knew I'd be here, so it was perfectly natural that he should ask me to make sure you were all right.'

'You mean make sure I lost the bet,' she flung at him, her tone accusing. To think she had nearly allowed herself to be lulled into letting him make love to her again. She could hardly believe she had been so gullible.

Her pain made her want to lash out and hurt in return. 'So what was the next move? Ask me to move in with you and then send the photos to my father?'

'Stop it,' he commanded. 'None of it was planned, and certainly not to sabotage your efforts. I didn't even know you were coming until I ran into your father at the solicitor's when I went to sign the lease. I hadn't seen him in months. He wanted to know what I was doing. When I told him, he explained about you coming here and asked me to make sure no harm came to you.'

Tears of frustration and disappointment clouded her vision, but she shook them off. 'Well, all I can say is, you did a lousy job of protecting me from harm. You've given Dad the perfect excuse to call the whole thing off. But I suppose that never occurred to you when you asked me to spend the night with you?'

He raked his hand through his hair, jumbling it into urchin spikes. 'Of course it didn't. That night the only thing on my mind was how much I wanted to make love to you. You didn't exactly try to fight me off.'

'Because I thought we belonged together. I should have known Dad would find a way to spoil things for me.'

'You make it sound as if he makes a habit of it.'

'It's an automatic response whenever I want to do something he disagrees with. I'm like a sheep that he has to herd back into the flock whenever I show signs of straying.'

Dane frowned. 'You're forgetting one thing. I'm not part of his flock, whatever you think. I told you I get what I want by fair means or not at all.'

She gave him a long look, filled with sadness. 'Then this time, it's not at all.'

'So you're going to hurt yourself before your father has a chance to do it, is that it?'

Was that what she was doing? She didn't know any more, and it was hard to think rationally when every instinct urged her to surrender to Dane's arms. They could take up where they had left off. Her senses were still vibrant with the need of him, so recently aroused and not yet satisfied.

But, even if Dane believed he was doing the right thing by agreeing to her father's wishes, she knew what the outcome would be. Her father would find a way to use Dane's presence against her. He didn't want her in the company. He wanted her safe and reliable at home, to look glamorous and play nursemaid to the Aunt Alices in his life.

She sighed aloud. Why would he give her up anyway, when she provided the one thing his money couldn't buy, domestic peace? Well, this time he had gone too far.

Dane watched the interplay of emotions on her face. 'I'm sorry it turned out this way,' he said with unexpected gentleness.

Her social conditioning helped her to keep the tears at bay as she faced him impassively. 'Why should you be sorry? You warned me how it would turn out. Aren't you thrilled to be proved right?'

Before he could answer, she spun around and walked quickly back along the path, heedless of the bushes which caught at her hair and clothing as she rushed onwards.

The others were lingering over coffee when she let herself into her cabin. The remains of their breakfast still littered the table. Jerry saluted her with a triangle of toast. 'We didn't wait for you. Julie thought you might have breakfast with Tarzan.'

About to correct him, she stopped herself. What did it matter what he called Dane? He was part of her past now, like Michael. 'I haven't eaten, but I'm not hungry,' she said.

Julie gestured with a cup and saucer. 'Coffee?'

'Thank you,' she said mechanically. She would have preferred to be by herself, but that would involve explanations she wasn't up to making right now. She sat down at the table.

Julie took note of her bright eyes and heightened colour. 'Is anything the matter? You look upset.'

'I'm fine, really. I did go to see Dane. You were right about him, Jerry. He's far from poor. I found out my father asked him to keep an eye on me while

I'm here.' Admitting it out loud made it painfully real, and her voice faltered as she spoke.

Concern brightened Julie's eyes. 'Does it make a difference to whether you get the job at CCI or not?'

She gave an elaborate shrug. 'Knowing my dad, he'll ensure it makes a difference.'

'He isn't playing fair.' Julie sounded shocked.

'Since when does Charlton Consett have to play fair?' she asked with brittle humour. 'He's determined to keep me at home where I can be the most use to him.'

'But what about when you get married? He'll have to lose you eventually.'

'The way things are going, marriage isn't all that likely, is it?'

Unable to keep up her pose of indifference any longer, she pushed her chair back and fled into the garden. She was relieved that her friends had the tact not to follow her. She didn't know which would be the harder to bear right now—Jerry's cruelty or Julie's sympathy.

She was relieved when the day ended and she could escort them to the jetty where Ned had arranged to pick them up. Jerry swayed slightly as he climbed aboard, having spiked his coffee with more rum from his bottomless supply. Ned gave him a wry look, but said nothing. 'Is there anything else you need until my next scheduled visit?' he asked, helping Julie aboard.

Evelyn passed him the last of the luggage. 'No, I have enough of everything,' she said. And more than enough of some things she didn't need, she added to herself. 'But you can tell my father that the telephone's out of order, in case he tries to reach me and gets worried.'

'So your phone *was* playing up, then? I'll tell your father and the phone people, so they can check the line.'

It didn't seem to matter one way or the other. 'There's nobody I want to phone,' she told him. 'There's no hurry.'

He glanced up at the sky and frowned. 'All the same, I don't like the idea of you being out of touch. There's going to be an almighty storm tonight.'

Her glance followed his. She had been so caught up in her problems that she hadn't noticed how ominously dark the sky had become. Perhaps it fitted in too well with her mood. 'I'll be all right,' she assured Ned.

'Then I can't persuade you to come back to Kettering with me?'

She shook her head. Staying the full month on the island had become an obsession. Even if her father reneged on his part of the deal, she was determined to see it through to the bitter end for her own sake.

By the time Ned's boat pulled out and the last of Julie's calls of farewell echoed faintly across the water as the distance widened between them, she was no longer so sure her decision was wise. The sky was black with rain clouds which hung low over the island like devilish frosting on a green cake. The first drops of rain caught her as she hurried back to her cabin.

She was soaked by the time she got inside, although the rain didn't come down in full force until she was a few feet from the cabin door. In minutes the temperature had dropped several degrees and she shivered.

Going upstairs to change, she noticed rain dripping through the shingled roof. If she hadn't been so stubborn, Dane would have mended it for her. Thinking of him, she set her mouth in a firm line and thrust a plastic bucket under the leak. He was probably waiting for her to seek his help. It would justify whatever her father was paying him. She was determined not to give either of them the satisfaction.

Dressed in a cosy sweater and dry jeans, she went around the cabin, tidying up after Julie and Jerry. They were used to having staff to look after them, and it would never occur to them to wash a plate or a cup after using it, or to fold their bedding away.

A wry smile tugged at her mouth. She had been the same when she'd got here. It had only taken her a couple of days to realise that, if she didn't do her own cleaning up, no one would do it for her.

By the time she'd finished the wind had risen to a howling climax which bent the trees double. Branches flew high in the air as if made of matchwood. She could hear the ocean crashing against the shoreline in mountainous waves. Ned was right. It was going to be an awful night.

She had just finished making herself a mug of cocoa when there was a crash of thunder, then the lights went out. A high-pitched shriek tore at the

air, and it took her a moment before realising the
sound came from her own throat.

Gingerly she felt her way to the table and put the
hot liquid down well away from the edge. Then she
groped her way to a chair and sat down. The flames
of her wood stove provided a welcome circle of
yellow light. Beyond it, eerie shadows reached out
elongated arms to her.

'It's only a storm. It will soon be over,' she told
herself. She could cope. Still, she drank her choc-
olate quickly and decided the best place to be was
in bed.

There was no question of undressing. The loft
was pitch black, illuminated by sporadic flashes of
lightning. By the light of one flash she was horrified to see that rainwater was already pouring over
the top of the bucket.

Moving carefully, she set off back downstairs in
search of more pots and pans to alternate with the
bucket. She was half-way down the stairs when a
deafening crash reverberated overhead. The room
lightened as a jagged tree branch ripped through
the roof, showering her with shingles. Rain pelted
into her upturned face.

As the full fury of the storm hurtled about her,
she took another step downwards. The falling debris
had smashed the step. Her feet met empty air and
she felt herself falling. Wildly she grabbed for the
handrail, but the timber was slick with rainwater
and her fingers skidded over it. She fell the rest of
the way, glancing painfully off the remaining steps,
until she landed at the bottom with one leg twisted
under her.

Hysterical laughter bubbled in her throat as she realised the irony of her situation. Her wish had been granted. She was alone. She could die, and no one would find out until it was too late.

CHAPTER EIGHT

EVELYN had no idea how long she lay at the foot of the stairs, dazed with shock and pain. Above her, the wind shrieked like a soul in torment and the rain sheeted down on her unprotected head.

When she attempted to stand, stabs of pain shot up her calf. With a cry she sank to the floor again and bit her lip against the throbbing in her damaged ankle. Suddenly independence was a curse, not a blessing.

The wind dropped abruptly and the silence sounded deafening without the banshee howls. Close to her came a skittering sound and she tensed, listening. It came again, closer this time. Wild-eyed, she strained to see through the blackness. Let it be anything, but not rats, she prayed. If one crawled over her she would die.

Claws and fur brushed her outstretched hand, and she made a mewing sound, too terrified even to scream. With all her might she kicked out with her good leg, aiming blindly into the darkness.

There was an all too human howl of dismay, then strong arms went around her. 'It's all right, it's me. You're safe now.'

'Dane! Thank heavens!' She clung to him, relief making her incoherent. 'I thought you were a rat,' she finally forced out between chattering teeth.

'That's a matter of opinion,' he said drily. 'Actually, it was Henrietta who found you. She was the rat you thought you heard. She ran off when you lashed out.'

As he talked, Dane's capable hands were exploring her legs. She gasped when he reached her damaged ankle. 'Can you feel your toes?' he asked, hearing her response.

She nodded, then realised he couldn't see her gesture. 'Everything works,' she affirmed. 'But it still hurts.'

He continued his gentle but thorough exploration. 'You haven't broken anything,' he said at last. 'I think the ankle's sprained or badly bruised. We'll know which when I get you back to my cabin.'

He lifted her easily and she linked her arms around his neck. After the horror of the night, it felt like heaven to be in his arms, feeling the warmth penetrating her sodden clothes. She rested her cheek against his chest, hearing his heartbeat pulsing strongly through his shirt. 'You're soaked through,' she said worriedly.

His hands brushed damp strands of hair off her forehead. 'Don't worry about me. When I heard the lightning strike, I headed straight over here. I didn't stop to put on a jacket.'

'Is that what happened?'

'It struck the old manna gum outside your window and brought the whole tree down. The roots must have been loosened by earlier storms. The bulk of it landed behind the house, but a branch crashed through your roof.'

'I'm glad you came,' she murmured. The rocking motion of his footsteps was making her sleepy.

In answer, he brushed his lips over her forehead. 'So am I, believe me.'

She must have dozed off then, only awakening when Dane set her down gently on the couch in his living-room. Blissful warmth washed over her from the flames leaping in the fireplace. She stretched out her hands to it. She had never felt so cold in her life. The chill seeped through her clothes and into her very bones.

Dane came back with an armful of towels which he dumped on to the couch beside her. 'You'd better get out of those wet clothes,' he advised.

When she didn't move, he reached for her shirt buttons and made an impatient noise when she recoiled automatically. 'This is no time for false modesty.'

'I know.' In any case, he had already seen her without any clothes at all. She couldn't explain her sudden feelings of shyness, even to herself.

He supplied his own explanation. 'It's Jerry, isn't it?'

Her gaze was uncomprehending. 'What?'

'You're regretting what happened between us because of him, aren't you?'

'No, I . . .'

'It's all right. I was the one who insisted on no strings, remember? You can let me take care of you on the same basis.'

He was utterly wrong about her and Jerry, but she was too bone weary to argue with him now. All she wanted was to be warm and to sleep. Explanations could wait. She made no further protests when he peeled off her sodden clothes and swathed her in warm towels.

'You'd better dry yourself,' he said hoarsely, standing up. 'I'll get a bed ready for you.'

Left alone, she began to dry herself with mechanical movements. Her sleepiness had evaporated with Dane's terse comments. It was clear that he didn't want to touch her. Maybe he was the one who regretted their earlier intimacy. She knew he didn't want any strings, so she was a fool to expect any.

Her mouth tightened into a grim line as she realised how close she had come to making that mistake. She was glad now that she hadn't set Dane straight about her relationship with Jerry. At least she had a face-saving way out.

By the time he returned, she was composed again. Her fragile poise almost came unstuck when he began to bathe her ankle in hot and cold bandages. Every time he touched her, the contact sent pulses of pleasurable energy arcing through her.

Despite her attempt to appear indifferent, he noticed her reactions. 'I'm not hurting you, am I?'

She shook her head. 'My ankle already feels better.' It was a pity she couldn't say the same about the rest of her, which ached with the need for his touch.

'It's only a bad bruise, so the compress should help,' he told her. 'You were lucky not to break anything when you fell.'

He might have been a doctor, assessing a patient's condition, she thought miserably. Her gaze went to the fur rug in front of the fire. Had they really made love there, or was it the product of her own wishful thinking? It was hard to reconcile his impersonal behaviour now with the tender lover in her mind. She reminded herself that it was a measure of his determination not to get involved.

He stood up and dropped the bandages into the bowl. 'I'll help you upstairs to bed. With rest, your ankle should be as good as new in a day or so.'

'Where will you sleep?' she asked, remembering the arrangements in her own cabin.

He misunderstood her concern. 'Not in the loft, if it's worrying you. I'll make up a bed on the couch down here.'

'I should sleep on the couch,' she protested.

'There's no need to be a martyr. I spend lots of nights down here anyway, studying the animals.'

Further arguments seemed futile, so she allowed him to help her upstairs and into bed. But it was a long time before she fell asleep. When she did, her dreams were plagued by furry creatures which ran rings around her and frustrated her attempts to get to Dane. In her dreams, he stood watching her with his arms folded, making no move to help her as the Tasmanian Devils gambolled around her legs.

She awoke to find the sun streaming into the room. It took her a few minutes to remember where she was, then she caught sight of Dane waiting beside the bed, a laden tray in his hands. 'I brought you some breakfast.'

She rubbed the sleep from her eyes. 'What time is it?'

'Two in the afternoon. I thought you needed the rest.'

He settled the tray across her knees. Without much appetite, she appraised the fruit juice, muesli and toast he had provided. She would have preferred to go back to sleep, rather than face a new day. Food had no appeal at all.

Because he seemed to expect it, she drank the fruit juice and was surprised at how good the cool liquid felt to her parched throat. He was still watching her, so she nibbled on a piece of toast.

'I could make you some eggs if you prefer it,' he offered. 'But I remembered that this was what you ate at home.'

She kept her lashes lowered so that he wouldn't see the surprise in her eyes. She was astonished that he remembered the small detail, but cautioned herself against reading anything into it.

'This is fine,' she murmured.

'Most of your clothes were soaked in the storm, so I've lent you a shirt until yours are dry,' he went on.

Without much interest, she looked at the red and white checked shirt he placed across the foot of the bed. 'Thank you. I'll return it later, after I've salvaged my own stuff.'

'You'll do no such thing!'

Startled, she looked up to find his eyes wide with annoyance. What had she said to provoke him? 'I'm sorry if I'm being a nuisance,' she said.

'You aren't being a nuisance. The storm wasn't your fault. But your cabin is uninhabitable. I went over there this morning to take a look at it. You can't move back in until I repair the roof and the stairs.'

'Why should you do that?'

'Because I feel responsible for what happened.'

She was confused. 'You just said the storm was nobody's fault.'

'I knew your roof was unsafe. I should have insisted on fixing it. If I had, the flying branch might not have done so much damage.'

'But I can't stay here,' she insisted. She had already spent two nights under Dane's roof. It was just the excuse her father needed to back out of their deal.

Dane misunderstood her concern. 'Jerry doesn't have to know you're here,' he assured her. 'I don't plan on telling him.'

'That's big of you,' she said, her tone sarcastic. 'But you may as well take me back to the mainland today.'

'I'm afraid I can't. After last night's storm, the seas are too big for my boat to handle. Jerry will have to do without you for a few days more.'

It was on the tip of her tongue to tell him that Jerry was the last person she would rush back to see. It was the prospect of spending more nights under Dane's roof, knowing that he was beyond her reach, which made her sick with misery. Even the knowledge that her father had already won their bet bothered her less than Dane's indifference.

But Dane was gone before she could tell him any of this, even had it been wise. She listened to his footsteps disappearing down the stairs, then set the tray aside and flung back the bedclothes.

Her ankle was still painful, but at least it supported her weight. She favoured it as she dressed. Her underwear was dry to put on, then she buttoned on the shirt Dane had left for her. With its long tail, it was practically a dress on her. She belted it with a length of cord she found on Dane's dresser. The sleeves had to be rolled back several times before they fitted.

Limping into the kitchen, she found Dane cutting sandwiches. 'You shouldn't be up. That ankle needs rest,' he said severely, without looking up. When she didn't reply, he lifted his head and his eyes darkened as he caught sight of her. His hand tightened on the knife.

She knew she looked like a teenager in his shirt. Her tanned legs were bare to the thighs and the turned-back sleeves emphasised her slight proportions. 'Will I do?'

His breathing quickened as he stabbed the knife into the bread. 'You look fine.'

'Only fine?' She couldn't keep the disappointment out of her voice. What she had hoped to achieve by appearing before him like this, she wasn't sure. It obviously wasn't working.

'All right, you look sexy as all hell,' he ground out. 'You fill that shirt in ways which take my breath away. Is that what you'd want Jerry to say if he were here?'

Her tongue flicked across her lips in a nervous gesture. 'Maybe it's what I want you to say.'

He threw the knife down with a clatter. 'Well, you're in for a disappointment. You do look sexy in my shirt. I'd be less than a man if you didn't turn me on dressed like that. But I'd also be less than a man if I did anything about it. You may have no scruples. I know Janice didn't. But I wouldn't do that to another man, because I know how it feels to be on the receiving end.'

'Damn it, I'm not in love with Jerry. I hate him,' she blurted out, sorry she had let him think otherwise, even briefly.

His look was sceptical. 'I saw how you behaved with him at the waterfall. If you were acting then, how can I be sure you aren't acting now?'

'If you cared for me, you'd know I'm not acting,' she threw at him. 'But you don't care for me, do you? You only care for yourself. At least you had the decency to warn me.' She spun around on her good leg and hobbled into the living-room, where she flung herself down on the couch.

The pattern of the next few days was set. Each morning Dane would bring her a light breakfast on a tray, then pack a lunch for himself and go off to work on her cabin. She protested that her ankle was well enough for her to look after herself, but to no avail. She finally decided that he preferred her to stay out of his way.

So she was surprised when he suggested that she come with him to see how the work was progressing. It was the first time since she moved in with him that he had given any sign of wanting her company.

'Are you sure I won't be in the way?' she asked diffidently.

'I wouldn't ask you if you were,' he assured her.

Her ankle was almost healed, but she watched her step as they followed the bush path to her cabin. Several times, Dane took her arm to steady her as they came to an obstacle. She was appalled at how readily her body responded to his touch. As she took note of her leaping pulses and rising temperature, she wondered that Dane himself could appear so unaffected.

She was relieved when they reached her cottage and he had no need to touch her any more. She moved a little away from him to give herself some breathing space. His sceptical gaze followed her and she knew he was reading quite the wrong motive into her actions.

'I won't bite. There's no need to jump aside,' he said, confirming her suspicion.

'I thought you'd prefer not to be touched,' she said. 'Considering the length you've been going to avoid me.'

His eyebrows tilted upwards. 'Isn't it what you want?'

'You made the rules,' she reminded him. 'An affair with no strings, I think you said.'

'Which turned out to be wise, under the circumstances,' he growled.

She gave up. If she insisted that what he saw between her and Jerry was an act, he would assume she was acting for him, too. It was no good wishing she hadn't given in to the temptation to flaunt Jerry at him. But she wished she hadn't confirmed Dane's worst suspicions about her.

Lost in thought, she forgot to look where she stepped. Her toe snagged in a tree root and she pitched forward. If it hadn't been for Dane's lightning reflexes, she would have sprawled full-length in the dust. 'Thanks,' she said shakily.

He kept his grip on her waist. 'Have you hurt your ankle again?'

'No. You caught me in time.'

'Would that I had.'

His low-voiced murmur drew her startled gaze. He wasn't referring to her, surely? His expression gave her no clues.

'You can let me go now,' she said huskily. 'I promise I'll watch my step from here on.'

'Sound advice for both of us,' he agreed. As if it cost him a great effort, he withdrew his arm, the fingers trailing across her back and sending shivers down her spine.

Her control wavered. 'Dane, I . . .'

He pressed two fingers to her lips, effectively silencing her. 'Don't make promises you can't keep.'

She moved her lips against his fingers and he dropped his hand as if burned. The gesture of withdrawal made her feel as if he had poured cold water over her. 'I wasn't about to make any promises, since you don't want to hear them,' she retorted. 'But I think you're the one who's afraid of making promises—in case someone expects you to keep them.'

An angry gleam sprang to his pale eyes and he folded his arms across his chest. 'Go on. Don't stop now.'

'Very well, since you asked for it. I think you're glad I have the same background as your ex-wife. It gives you the perfect excuse to love me and leave me. No strings, indeed! What you really mean is "no responsibility accepted".'

Anger flared around him like an aura, so vivid that she was surprised not to see sparks shooting from his finger when he pointed it at her. 'I've had my share of responsibility, more than you'll ever be asked to shoulder.'

'You're forgetting how much you've told me about yourself,' she reminded him. 'Someone who walks off a family farm to make big money, then turns his back on that, and ditches his wife when she doesn't measure up—it isn't my idea of a responsible man.'

His control went and she gasped with shock when he took hold of her arms and propelled her towards her cabin. She fought his grip. 'Let me go, you bully.'

'When I've answered your charges,' he assured her, still steering her towards the cottage. He didn't release her until they were inside. Then he guided her to the rocking-chair and sat her down on it. She started to get up, but saw his thunderous expression and subsided again. 'All right, I'm listening,' she said, hoping she didn't sound as intimidated as she felt. What on earth had possessed her to throw such accusations at him when she knew so little about his background or his marriage?

He propped himself against the mantelpiece. Behind him she could see the gleam of new timber where he had rebuilt the staircase. The roof had been mended overhead, too, but he gave her no time to appreciate his handiwork. 'When I have your attention,' he said with heavy sarcasm.

She pulled her eyes back to him. 'Sorry.'

He held up his hand, fingers extended. 'Point one,' he said, ticking it off, 'I didn't walk off the family farm, as you suggested. My parents had a small goat-breeding concern in the Derwent Valley. Dad inherited the land from his father, but instead of running sheep, he turned it over to pure-bred Saanen goats.'

A nostalgic smile lit her face. 'I've seen them on my holidays in the valley. They're the goats with the pointed ears that stand up. The kids have dazzling white coats like newborn lambs.'

'Only the purebreds have those ears,' he told her. 'You must have seen them on my Dad's farm.'

'He moved away, didn't he?' she asked as another memory came back. Then she gnawed on the tip of her thumb. 'Our neighbours bought him out, didn't they?'

'Ten out of ten,' he said sarcastically. 'But they weren't bought out. They were forced out.'

She jumped to her feet. 'That's not true. The Drummonds paid a high price for the land so that they could expand their breeding programme.'

'No doubt they told it differently, but they gave my parents no option but to sell out. They bought up all the surrounding land, including the water supply my parents depended on.'

She felt the colour leave her face as she realised what Dane's family had gone through. She had assumed that they left willingly, well compensated for the loss of land. She had never dreamed that the sale was forced. 'I'm sorry, I didn't know,' she said in a low voice.

He shrugged. 'Why should you? It was no concern of yours. Your father bought out quite a few smallholdings in the valley in his time. I don't blame him for wanting to increase his holdings. In his shoes, I'd probably have done the same thing.'

Her head swung violently from side to side. 'No, you wouldn't. You aren't like that.'

The pale eyes were hooded and seemed almost dark as they rested on her. 'I wasn't, but I nearly became like that, which I count the worst crime of all. He moved restlessly, as if it troubled him to remember what had happened. 'When I saw my parents forced into retirement they didn't want, I made up my mind never to be powerless again. I decided to amass a fortune large enough to protect my own. I even chose my wife because she could be an asset to me in my climb.

'Don't look so stricken,' he added when he saw her horrified reaction. 'She was happy with the deal at first. She liked being married to the boy wonder of the futures board, who could give her everything her heart desired. We were a good team because both of us had priorities which didn't include love.'

'But you couldn't go on like that,' she anticipated, astonished to find that she had misjudged him so completely.

'I thought I could, but I couldn't. I wanted to be ruthless and grasping, but I couldn't live with myself. I made a fortune all right, but it was an empty victory.'

'But lots of successful men are philanthropists,' she interrupted. 'They're not all cold and calculating.'

His mouth twisted into a cynical smile. 'Maybe, but there's usually a tax benefit or an ego trip behind it, or so I found. Rather than try to change the nature of the beast, I decided to opt out.'

'But Janice didn't share your enthusiasm?' He had already told her that much.

'When I told her I wanted more from life and asked her to share my plans, she laughed in my face. She took the greatest pleasure in telling me she'd been having an affair with her retail baron for years behind my back. If I hadn't been working sixteen hours a day for her and for my own particular demons, I might have found out sooner. Still, she was surprised when I wished her well on my way out.'

It was hardly the picture of Dane she had been compiling since they met. But it was more in tune with the man he seemed to be. She could imagine him setting out to make himself financially invulnerable, and it seemed he had succeeded. But she also understood, better than he knew, how bleak life could be when all you had was a fortune.

'I'm glad you told me,' she said softly. 'I'm sorry for the things I said.'

His eyes flashed challenging fire. 'As long as you're not sorry for me. For better or worse, I chose my own path.'

The idea of feeling sorry for Dane was so absurd that she almost laughed aloud, but she didn't want him to think she was laughing at him so she fought the temptation. She stood up. If she stayed beside him a moment longer, sharing his confidences, she would break down and tell him how much he meant to her.

'This is getting too serious,' she said, injecting a light note into her voice. 'Weren't you going to show me your handiwork?'

'I should get my priorities right, shouldn't I?' he said coldly.

She recoiled from the implied rebuke. She hadn't meant him to think his confessions weren't important to her. 'I didn't mean...' she began.

'Forget it,' he cut in before she could finish. 'Let's start with the staircase.'

Heart-sore, she followed him around the cabin, duly admiring the new woodwork. In daylight, she was shocked to see how much damage the storm had done to the cottage. The extent of the new work could be seen clearly in the roof. She had been lucky not to be killed, either by flying debris or by the fall.

She shivered and wrapped her arms around herself. 'I didn't realise how bad the damage was.'

'I told you the place was uninhabitable. I'm not in the habit of lying.'

He was determined to take everything she said the wrong way. 'I know,' she said on a sigh. 'I just didn't think it was as bad as this. You've done a wonderful job of repairing the place.'

'It had to be done,' he said dismissively. 'One benefit of growing up on a farm is being able to turn your hand to most manual tasks.'

'Do you miss the land?' she asked.

His hard expression lightened a fraction. 'Sometimes. I might buy back the old farm one of these days. I've often thought about it.'

She found herself hoping he would, and wondered if she should say something to her father. The Drummonds, who had bought Dane's old place, were friends of Charlton Consett's. Surely he could persuade them to part with the land? Then she realised it was the very opposite of what Dane would want. She risked a sidelong glance at him. If he wanted the land, he was capable of getting it without her help or patronage.

She noticed a leather-bound book lying at the foot of the stairs. 'What's this?'

'I found it under the debris. It's a diary. I didn't read it in case it was personal.'

Opening it, she recognised her mother's looping copperplate handwriting. The shock of seeing it made her vision blur for a moment before she had herself back under control. 'It's my mother's,' she told Dane. 'She must have kept it when she was staying on the island.'

'Did you know she kept a diary?'

She shook her head. 'She never said anything, but I can understand why she would. Whenever she talked about Frere Island, Dad switched off. You could see him doing it.'

'Since he couldn't develop it or exploit it, he probably didn't see any point in discussing it,' Dane assumed.

It stung Evelyn, but she had to admit he was right. It was the reason why Lorna Consett spent so much time here alone. Evelyn hugged the journal to her. She could hardly wait to read it. It would be like having her mother back again for a brief time. She turned shining eyes to Dane. 'Thank you for finding it.'

He seemed uncomfortable with her raw emotions. 'If it hadn't been for the stairs collapsing, it would have been lost for good.'

She wished he would accept at least some of the credit, but he seemed determined not to, just as he was determined not to accept any of the love she wanted to offer him. 'All the same, I'm grateful.'

He moved towards the door and rested his hand on the knob. 'At least you'll have it to occupy you while I'm gone.'

Her surprise was ill disguised, and she had to fight a moment of panic at the thought that he might be leaving for good. 'Gone where?' she asked.

He brushed his hair back with a careless gesture. 'I've been worried about my boat, but I haven't had any time to check on it since the storm.'

Because he had been too busy repairing her cabin, she guessed, feeling a pang of guilt. 'Aren't the seas too rough?' she asked, recalling why he couldn't take her back to Hobart before.

'They've abated enough to move the boat. If I keep to the shelter of the island, it should be OK.'

She set the journal aside and dusted off her palms. 'Can I come with you?'

'It might be rough,' he cautioned.

Rough or not, she couldn't let him go alone. Any trial would be easier than waiting for him to return.

'I don't care,' she said decisively. 'I'm coming with you.'

CHAPTER NINE

As HE led the way through the tangled undergrowth which choked the centre of the island, Dane was so morose that it was obvious he resented her presence. He made no allowances for her damaged ankle as he forged ahead.

'I thought you said it wasn't far,' she said, pushing aside the branches which threatened to snap across her face.

He glanced back over his shoulder. 'It's a forty-minute walk. At low tide you can walk along the beach, but the tide will be in now so we have to go through the bush.'

'What's the hurry?' she asked. It was becoming more and more of an effort not to limp.

A frown crossed his face, but he slowed his pace somewhat and regarded her critically when she caught up. 'Are you sure you're up to a long hike yet?'

'I'll be fine if you only slow down,' she insisted.

'I'm afraid we can't. There's another storm blowing up, and I want the boat safely moored at the jetty before the seas get too high.'

She leaned against a tree, enjoying the brief respite. 'Why didn't you use the jetty in the first place?'

'Friar's Cove is more secluded. Most boats pass the island on this side. Having a boat at the jetty tends to advertise your presence.'

'No wonder Ned thought the island was deserted. You wanted people to think so, until I came along and spoiled your retreat.'

He gave her a hard look which revealed little. 'Disturbed is the better word than spoiled,' he said.

You could disturb someone for better or for worse, she considered, although she had little doubt that he meant the latter. 'Well, you needn't worry, I'll be gone soon,' she said.

His eyebrows arched into a V of surprise. 'The month isn't up yet.'

'It might as well be,' she said diffidently. 'The day I moved into your cabin, I as good as forfeited the bet. At least, my father will think so.'

'Do you mind?'

There was a silence while she thought. 'When I came here, getting a job with CCI seemed like life or death. Now it no longer seems so important. There are other places I can work.'

'Won't your name be a hindrance?' She had already told him about her experience with the real estate company.

'I thought about that. All I have to do is work under another name. Authors do it all the time.' Some imp of mischief made her add. 'How does Evelyn Balkan sound?'

His angry look seared her. 'Don't play games with me, Evelyn. Having a woman take my name implies a serious commitment. It isn't a joking matter.'

Had she been joking when she suggested it? The name sprang so easily to her lips that she wondered about it.

'I guess it was a stupid thing to say,' she said with more than a hint of double meaning.

He straightened and brushed the leaves from his jeans where he had been leaning against a tree. 'We'd better get moving.'

When he started off down the path, she tested her weight on her ankle. A twinge of warning pain travelled up her calf. She sat down again. 'It's no good. I can't go on.'

At once he doubled back. 'I was wondering when you'd admit defeat.'

She reached down and massaged her ankle. 'Go ahead and gloat.'

He sobered. 'I'm not gloating. As a matter of fact, I admire your courage. But you don't have to come. You can wait for me back at the cabin. I'll be home in time for dinner.'

Home in time for dinner. It sounded so cosily domestic that she almost wished he meant it that way. But he was only being kind. 'I feel so useless,' she complained.

Touching a hand under her chin, he pressed gently so she looked up at him. 'You're not useless,' he said firmly. 'You've shown you can handle it. You don't have to prove a thing to anyone else.'

His gaze held her captive until she lowered her lashes over suddenly moist eyes. 'Thanks,' she said huskily.

He helped her to her feet. 'Can you get back to the cabin under your own steam?'

'Yes, if I take it slowly.'

'Very well, I'll go for the boat. Take care.' He dropped the lightest of kisses on to her forehead, then strode off through the bush, the greenery closing behind him like a curtain.

She waited until he was out of sight, then retraced her steps to the path which led to Dane's cabin. From what she had seen this morning, there was no reason why she shouldn't move back into her own cabin, but she resisted the idea. Telling herself that Dane still had more work to do on her place, she turned towards his cottage.

By the time she reached it, the wind was noticeably stronger and the sky was dotted with grey-rimmed clouds. She hoped Dane wouldn't get caught in the storm. He had explained that his boat was an ex-Navy launch and quite capable of putting out to sea, but the diesel engine still needed work. When she asked why he hadn't bought a new cruiser in perfect condition, he said he enjoyed the challenge of restoring the old vessel.

She recalled how enthusiastically he had described the boat. 'Thirty foot and made of splendid old Huon pine. You can't get timber like that any more.'

How could she ever have accused him of running away from responsibility? Even in his choice of boat, he had refused to take the easy way out.

Without Dane, the cabin felt lonely and unwelcoming. It was a feeling she'd better get used to. He was determined to exclude her from his life. His reaction when she linked her name with his was surely proof.

She tried to tell herself it was for the best. He had betrayed her by teaming up with her father behind her back. Yet her body persisted in remembering how glorious his lovemaking felt. After the warmth of his arms, the world seemed suddenly much colder.

It *was* colder, she realised with a shock. While she'd been daydreaming, the temperature had dropped several degrees, foreshadowing a cold evening ahead. Dane would be back before then, she told herself, and set about making up the fire. If only her father could see her now, deftly preparing the kindling so that it would catch the larger logs. She was almost an expert at it now.

For all the good it would do her, she thought soberly. Lighting fires, cooking meals and keeping house were skills most women took for granted. They were hardly marketable. And although her words to Dane about changing her name had been light-hearted, the underlying intent was serious. If she had to use another name in order to be accepted on her own merits, then that was what she would do.

What would Dane do when he left here? she found herself wondering. He had talked about setting up the wildlife sanctuary here. He certainly had a way with the animals. He hadn't mentioned the idea again after she'd suggested that he stay on the island and run the project. Her offer had been genuine, but he'd chosen to see it as some kind of patronage. Oddly enough, although his stubborn pride frustrated her, it also pleased her. He was his own man and she admired him for that.

The fire was crackling merrily and she sat back, wondering how best to pass the time until Dane returned. A pot of thick vegetable soup stood ready for their evening meal, and she had baked fresh damper that morning, so dinner would require little preparation.

Then she remembered her mother's journal which Dane had retrieved from under the stairs in her cottage. It lay on the table where they had left it before setting off for the boat. Now she picked it up, caressing the worn leather cover as if it were her mother's hand. She still missed her mother, even after ten years. With a sigh, she opened the journal at random.

'Today I brought Lindy to the island for the first time,' the entry began. Evelyn stared at it in fascination. No one had called her Lindy since she was a little girl.

'Lindy particularly enjoyed seeing the Tasmanian Devils which come up to feed at dusk. I'll never forget her enchanted expression.'

Evelyn looked up. Her mother's words had conjured up a memory of that night, the first she had spent on the island. Her father had been away on a business trip and Alex was at boarding-school. Little did either of them know that the next time she fed the animals it would be in the company of a man who was half-devil himself. All the same, she had a feeling her mother would have approved of Dane. He shared her belief in conservation and her love of the wild.

'Ever since I inherited this place from my mother, I have cherished a dream of seeing it set aside as a refuge for the animals where people can enjoy seeing them in their natural surroundings,' her mother wrote. 'Charlton says people would abuse my trust if I put the island to such use. Without his help, I can't do more than dream. Perhaps things will be different when Lindy's grown up.'

As a flood of emotions overwhelmed her, Evelyn closed the book. As a young married woman, her mother had been bound by convention to follow her husband's wishes. Although she'd come to the marriage with a sizeable fortune of her own, it had been expected that Charlton would manage it for her and provide for her needs.

But things *were* different for Evelyn, she realised, her eyes starting to shine. With the backing of her father's advisors, she had managed her own trust fund since she was twenty-one. Even if her father still didn't approve of the venture, she could make her mother's dream come true.

A scratching sound outside the door startled her. At first she thought it was the wind, blowing branches back and forth across the cabin wall. When it came again she was frightened, until she remembered that the Tasmanian Devils were expecting their evening meal. Her gaze flew to the kitchen clock. It was getting late, and still there was no sign of Dane.

Mechanically, she got out the shredded meat for the animals and divided it among the tin plates Dane used to feed them. They clustered around her, growling and snarling and competing for space as she set the plates down on the ground.

'Stop that, there's plenty for everyone,' she chided them. She knew now that the snarling was good-natured and rarely led to serious fighting. She noticed that Henrietta was first in line to be fed. She ruffled the animal's coarse fur. 'Thanks for saving my life,' she said softly.

Dark eyes shining, the animal looked up at her as if in acknowledgement, then gave all its attention to the food.

Satisfied that the bounty was distributed fairly, she moved away from the feeding animals. Their cries followed her as she walked to the edge of the clearing. Beyond the well of light cast by the cabin, there was only blackness. The wind made a keening noise as it threaded its way through the trees. Overhead, the thick banks of cloud scudded back and forth across the sky. She shivered, imagining the wind whipping the seas around the island into a frenzy. Where on earth was Dane?

When the evening wore on and there was still no sign of him, she began to pace up and down, her arms wrapped around herself in pale imitation of his touch. She should do something, but what? She didn't even know exactly where his boat was moored, far less which route he planned to take to reach the jetty.

She stopped in her tracks. Ned Freils could help her. Dane had told her that the telephone was working again, so she could call Ned from her cabin. She hated to ask the old man to put to sea in such awful weather, but there was nothing else she could do.

Favouring her ankle, she set off down the bush path, lighting her way by the thin beam of a torch she had brought from the cabin. The wind was ripping so many branches from the trees that she was afraid of being knocked down and had to keep dodging debris along the path.

So far the rain had held off, but suddenly it came sheeting down with such force that she was soaked through in seconds. Bent forwards, she strained to see through the torrential downpour. It was useless. The storm was so fierce that she was in danger of losing her way. In these conditions she could easily injure her ankle again or wander into the lagoon. What use would she be to Dane then? Reluctantly she retraced her steps to his cabin.

The animals, wiser in the ways of nature than she was, had retreated to their hollow logs and other hiding places to wait out the storm. She had no choice but to do the same.

Inside the cabin, she curled up on Dane's couch and wrapped a blanket around her shoulders. If the storm showed any signs of easing she would try again to reach her cabin.

She wasn't aware of falling asleep until she was jolted awake by a crashing sound on the roof. She looked up in time to see a huge tree branch come hurtling through the roof, showering her with debris. The rain poured in through the gaping hole.

'Oh, please, not again,' she whimpered, huddling into her blanket. Then she realised that the blanket was dry, despite the water pouring down on her. She looked around in wonder. She was back home in her room at Battery Point, and light was streaming in from a hole in the ceiling.

The rain had stopped and a family of Tasmanian Devils were play-fighting on her bed. As she watched them her sense of bewilderment grew. The largest animal was Henrietta. She recognised the star-shaped white ruff around the animal's dark neck. She had a baby clinging to her back. It was trying to reach her pouch to feed, and Henrietta was making growls of irritation through widely gaping jaws.

Suddenly there was a blinding flash of lightning and more tree branches began to fall from the hole in the roof. Afraid that Henrietta and her baby would be hurt, Evelyn struggled to get to them, but her ankle refused to support her. Her whirling thoughts focused on one thing. If Dane were here, everything would be all right.

Still struggling to reach the animals which were squealing in terror, she began to call Dane's name over and over until she was screaming it. Her throat felt raw, but she kept it up. She had to make him hear. Then something grabbed her and she had to fight that too. 'Dane, where are you? Help me, please,' she called, her voice trailing off into a sob.

Miraculously, he answered. 'It's all right, I've got you. It's only a dream. I'm here.'

The room swam into focus and she found herself on his couch with his arms tightly around her. He was stroking her hair and murmuring her name over and over. His eyes were wide with concern.

Bewildered, she looked around. The roof was intact and there was no sign of the animals. She must have dreamed it all. 'It was the storm. I thought it was destroying everything,' she said hoarsely.

'It was a pretty bad squall, but it's over now,' he assured her. 'It brought back memories of your fall and gave you the nightmare. But everything's all right.'

The intensity of the dream faded and she began to feel foolish. 'I was so worried about you,' she said. 'What happened?'

'The engine played up so I was late setting off from Friar's Cove. I thought I would beat the storm, but it blew up so suddenly and so fiercely that I had to put into the first sheltered bay until it was safe to go on.'

'I thought you had been blown out to sea or...or been swamped,' she said shakily. 'It was awful not knowing. I tried to go to the telephone to call Ned Freils for help.'

He touched the damp strands of her hair. 'So that's how you got so wet.'

'You're rather soggy yourself,' she observed, noticing how his shirt and jeans clung to him, outlining every muscle of his superb body. The wet clothes set her errant imagination racing and her pulses began to leap in response. 'You'd better get out of those wet clothes,' she said, sounding huskier than she intended.

Her stomach muscles tightened as she watched his eyes grow dark with passion. He seemed to be fighting an internal battle with himself. She was aware of the exact moment that he lost the battle, because her body went haywire at the same time.

The sudden fluttering of her heart matched the quickening of his breath as he leaned towards her.

'Dear heaven, Evelyn. Out in the storm, all I could think of was getting back to you.'

'I kept thinking of you too. If anything had happened...'

He saw the panic in her eyes and quelled it with the pressure of his mouth on hers.

The storm raging outside was nothing compared to the one which he triggered inside her. Her emotions, already close to the surface, overwhelmed her. Wrapping her arms around his neck, she kissed him with desperate passion until she felt as if they must fuse into one molten being.

Dane was like a man possessed. He showered her face and neck with hot kisses, his lips feverish and his eyes blazing. His fingers, usually so deft, fumbled on the buttons of her shirt, but he got it open at last. Her breasts felt swollen and tender, the roseate peaks sensitised so that when he took each one in his mouth in turn she felt light-headed with her need of him.

This was no ordinary passion. The night had torn them away from each other. Through his love-making, Dane was returning to her. She clung to him with a fervour she had never experienced before. When he tilted her back against the couch and stood up to remove his wet clothing, she had to fight the urge to cling to him, never to let him go.

When he came to her, she embraced him with every part of her, spreading her hands across his back to encompass as much of him as was possible.

She had never known such need, and it drove her to sensations beyond her wildest imaginings.

Around the cabin the wind howled and raged on, but it couldn't compete with her inner storm as Dane drove her higher and higher. Willingly, she soared with him on the wings of loving joy, right into the eye of the storm.

Slowly, slowly, she became aware of other sensations: his damp skin hot against hers; the musky male scent of him filling her nostrils; and the tandem pounding of their hearts as normality seeped back.

She buried her face in his shoulder. The magic of the moment was too precious and fragile to be dissipated with mere words, so she contented herself with murmuring his name over and over.

Lifting his head, he kissed her gently, then lay on his side behind her. The narrow couch pressed them closely together, so they nestled spoon fashion. As his arm grew heavy around her waist, she sighed with contentment. Surely, after this, he must see that they belonged together?

Reaching down, she pulled the blanket up so that it covered them both. Outside, the noise of the storm gradually abated. Inside, it was already over and she revelled in its aftermath of blissful contentment.

When she awoke, the sun was shining and Dane was gone. If it hadn't been for the imprint his head had left in the cushion, she could have imagined last night. She hadn't, had she?

Stretching her cramped limbs, she was aware of aches in muscles she didn't normally use. No, she hadn't imagined any of last night, but she might have misconstrued it.

In the clear light of day, she saw Dane's love-making for what it must be, a source of comfort they had both desperately needed. She was glad he wasn't here to see the chagrin she felt for reading too much into it.

Slowly, she got up, washed and dressed. The wood-fired bath heater held no terrors for her any more. She smiled when she remembered her early battles with it. What a long way she had come.

The thought was some solace as she made coffee and toast for breakfast. When Dane didn't come back, she made some of the toast into sandwiches with bacon for him, wrapped them in a clean tea towel and went in search of him.

As she'd expected, he was at her cabin, putting the finishing touches to the repaired staircase. For some reason, he seemed angry. He planed and sanded the timber with savage intensity. She realised she must be right about last night.

'Good morning,' she said softly, drawing his attention.

'Is it?' he asked softly, then bent to his work again.

'Look, if it was something I said...'

He dropped the tool with a clatter. 'No, it's me. I feel like a heel after last night.'

'Why? Just because you made love to me, I don't expect a lifetime commitment.' He had already made it clear he wasn't offering any such thing.

His pale gaze was as bleak as a winter landscape. 'Is that supposed to make me feel better?'

'It's supposed to be the truth. You wouldn't want me swearing undying love, would you?' She laced her words with sarcasm so that he wouldn't suspect that it was the very thing her heart yearned to do.

He gave her a searching look. 'You'd better stick to the truth.'

His truth, she thought miserably. He had warned her against falling in love with him, and he would be horrified if she told him now. She was the one who had changed, not Dane.

She unwrapped the sandwiches and gave them to him. Without comment, he ate one, then was about to bite into another when he paused. 'There was a telephone call for you this morning. Jerry rang. He was surprised that you weren't here.'

'Did you tell him where I was?'

'I thought that was up to you. Will you tell him?'

'Of course not.' If Jerry knew, he might say something to her father, and she preferred to tell him herself.

Dane's mouth tightened into a grim line. 'I see. What he doesn't know won't hurt him.'

'No,' she protested. 'I don't care what Jerry thinks.'

'Of course you don't. Why should you?' He parcelled up the remaining sandwiches and set them aside, then stood up. 'I'm going outside for some air.'

A cold feeling settled over her. He thought she was cheating on Jerry and didn't care as long as she wasn't caught, just like his ex-wife. She was about to follow him outside and try to explain, when the telephone rang.

'It's you again,' she said when she recognised Jerry's voice.

'Yes, it's me, but you're talking to a reformed man.'

He sounded sober and sensible, but she was still suspicious. 'In what way?'

'In every way. Your island must have some magic in the air. I woke up the morning after my visit and faced the fact I was throwing my life away on booze, drugs and having a good time. With the exception of the last bit, I've given them all up. Besides, I'm getting married.'

'Married?' she echoed. 'I don't believe it.'

'Believe it. Last night, Sandy Cabot agreed to become my wife.'

Evelyn remembered Sandra as a petite blonde who had graced Jerry's arm on many occasions. Jerry's dalliances with other girls, herself included, had blinded everyone to the fact that he kept going back to Sandra. Now the reason was clear. 'That's marvellous,' she enthused.

'I'm glad you're pleased, because Sandy and I want you to come to the wedding.'

'I accept,' she said, with a catch in her voice. 'Julie must be so pleased.'

'She is. But it's mostly relief at having me off the family's hands.'

'I'm sure you're wrong. Love changes people.' She, of all people, knew that.

'Even me,' he agreed. 'Well, I wanted you to be the first to know. Also I wanted to ask whether we can honeymoon on Frere Island, since it's where I came to my senses.'

'Of course. I can't think of a better place for a honeymoon.'

'You're an angel. You make me sorrier than ever for treating you so badly before.'

'Forget it. It's in the past,' she urged. Holding a grudge was totally foreign to her nature. She was just glad that Jerry had woken up to himself in time.

A sound outside made her turn. Through a window she saw Dane striding away from the cabin. His back was ramrod straight and his strides were long and decisive. He was heading for the jetty.

Without knowing why, she felt uneasy. It was difficult to concentrate on Jerry's rambling account of doings at home. 'I'm sorry, what did you say?' She forced herself to concentrate on his voice.

'I asked whether you had any news of your own. I've been trying to call you for two days, and Julie's dying of curiosity.'

'My phone's been out of order,' she said. It was the truth.

He chuckled throatily. 'Then your father was wrong. He thinks your roof blew off and you moved in with Balkan. I have my doubts about the roof part.' For a moment, he sounded like the Jerry Cummings of old, until he added, 'Sorry. I shouldn't have said that.'

She ignored the apology. 'Has Dad been spying on me?'

'You'd know better than me, love. There's only one phone there and it's yours. Julie and I didn't say anything, I swear, so who does that leave?'

She knew exactly who it left. Dane didn't have a telephone but he did have a boat. He must have used his radio to report to her father. No one else knew about the storm damage.

Her legs felt weak and she clung to the kitchen counter-top for support. How could Dane do this to her? He had denied he was working for her father. She had believed him and this was how he had repaid her trust.

'Are you still there?'

'Yes, Jerry, but I have to go. I must call my father.' She had no hope of salvaging their deal now. Dane had put paid to that. But she wanted to tell her side of the story.

'What will you do if you don't get a job with CCI?' Jerry asked her.

'You mean when,' she said glumly. 'I didn't last a month by myself, so Dad's entitled to claim victory. I'm not sure it's so important now. I've learned a lot about myself since I came here, and I've made a few plans of my own.'

'As I said, your island has an odd effect on people.'

She repeated her good wishes to Jerry, then they said their goodbyes and she hung up. The island had worked its magic on Jerry, but had had the opposite effect on her. She had become self-sufficient in ways that seemed trivial now, when she counted the cost. In Dane, she had found a man to love, honour and cherish. Yet he had betrayed her, admittedly with plenty of warning. It was little consolation.

Distantly she heard an engine starting up. Her body acted independently of her will, taking her along the bush path towards the jetty before she fully realised where she was going.

When she got there, Dane's boat was already well out into the bay. She could just make out his broad-shouldered form at the helm. He did not look back.

She shouldn't be surprised to see him go. He'd done what her father paid him to do and was now free to leave. Her mouth twisted into a wry smile as she thought of what her father would say if he knew how thoroughly Dane had carried out his assignment.

Her smile became bitter and tears stung the backs of her eyes. It was the one thing she was sure Dane would never tell him.

CHAPTER TEN

EVELYN thought what an incongruous picture she must make. Dressed in a eucalypt-green Carla Zampatti trouser-suit, she had her sleeves rolled up and was covered in flour to her elbows. She was making a deep-dish pie of chunky meat and vegetables topped with pastry, from a recipe found in her mother's journal.

The domestic illusion would have been complete but for the ache inside her which refused to go away. Two days had passed since Dane had left without a word. She was forced to accept that he might not come back.

With a heavy heart, she had taken over the task of feeding the colony of Tasmanian Devils. It gave her an excuse to visit Dane's cottage each day. Just being among his things made her feel closer to him. It was hard to believe that he had simply walked out, leaving everything behind, yet she knew he put so little value on possessions that it was all too possible.

She had tried to reach her father without success. He was away. Even his secretary, Donna Radcliffe, couldn't help. It was some consolation that, if she couldn't reach Charlton, Dane couldn't either, with his damning report.

Where was Dane now? She ached to know. It was crazy since he was obviously on her father's side, but the memory of his lovemaking burned inside her like an eternal flame. She could feel it consuming her spirit. Soon there would be only ashes left.

With a floury hand, she pushed back the strands of lemon-meringue hair which strayed across her eyes. Damn Dane Balkan for his treachery. And for being so easy to love.

Outside it was a glorious spring day. The sky was an impossible blue high overhead, and the sun made dappled patterns on the forest floor. Already, her transplanted garden was budding. Soon a carpet of wild boronia would surround the cabin.

The only sound was the ever-present ocean beyond the trees, the noisy squabbles of the yellow wattle birds and the occasional screech of a white cockatoo which had taken to visiting her garden.

The sounds soothed her troubled spirit. She punctuated them with the thurrump of the pastry as she kneaded and turned it.

Gradually she became aware of another sound intruding on her senses. It grew louder until she recognised it as a boat pulling into the bay.

In spite of herself, her heart leapt and swallowing became difficult. She refused to let herself think as she rinsed the flour from her hands and hurried out of the cabin.

But the boat pulling into the jetty wasn't a battered ex-Navy launch. It was Ned Freils' charter boat. Disappointment knifed through her as she recognised Ned's passenger.

'Permission to come ashore,' her father called as Ned brought the boat close in to the jetty.

'Hello, Dad,' she said dully. 'Of course you can come ashore.'

Ned brought the boat alongside the wooden pier and let it idle until Charlton Consett had jumped off. With a wave to her, Ned took the boat out again, not even bothering to tie up.

Father and daughter watched until the sound of Ned's engines died away and the backwash subsided, then Charlton turned to her. 'Surprised to see me?'

'Not really,' she admitted. Dane had obviously managed to make his report, prompting Charlton to claim his victory in person. Nevertheless, she recognised that, despite everything, she was pleased to see her father. 'Come up to the cabin,' she invited.

With the air of a lord inspecting his fiefdom, he strolled alongside her, his sharp eyes noting every change she had made. 'You've done a lot since you got here. This garden was a real jungle.'

'I had to do something with my time,' she said, pride creeping into her voice.

'Your mother would be happy to see the place looked after. I kept thinking I ought to send some workmen over, but I never got around to it.'

'Luckily for me, or I'd have had nothing to do.'

'You would have found something,' her father said, giving her a shrewd look.

Inside the cabin, Charlton caught sight of the pastry-making project and chuckled. 'Mrs Godfrey had better look to her laurels.'

Sarah Godfrey was her father's housekeeper. 'I don't think she has much to worry about. My pastry still tastes like shoe-leather,' Evelyn said. 'But I'm trying.'

He sobered. 'So I hear.'

Now they were coming to it. 'What do you hear?' she asked with studied casualness.

'How well you've been doing. I saw Julie and Jerry after they came to visit, and they had nothing but praise for your efforts.'

Bless them, she thought. She tensed, waiting for the rest. 'And?'

'And I could use some of that coffee you're brewing. It smells delicious.'

Fuming with impatience, but knowing her father wouldn't be hurried, she made coffee for him. When she cut him a slice of her home-made damper, still warm from the oven, he was full of praise for her home-making skills.

'I suppose you're trying to tell me I should stick to home and hearth, after all,' she forestalled him.

His eyebrows arched in surprise. 'Not at all. I was only giving credit where I feel it's due.'

She couldn't contain herself any longer. 'Dad, I know why you're here. Dane Balkan was in touch with you, wasn't he?'

He set his cup down on the table. 'Yes, he was. But he wasn't supposed to spoil my surprise.'

She could hardly call it a surprise. 'He didn't have to,' she said heavily. 'I already know I lost the bet.'

His mouth twitched in amusement. 'Do you, now? Well, I suppose we did agree that you were to fend for yourself. You could hardly do that under another man's roof.'

'So he told you I moved in with him?'

'Yes. He also told me about the storm and your roof falling in, which was the reason you couldn't stay here. Good heavens, girl, you could have been killed. As it was, you were hurt. I blame myself for letting it happen.'

'You didn't let it happen,' she said tiredly. 'I insisted on coming here. You had nothing to do with it.'

He brushed his thick silver hair back with a sweeping gesture. 'I know, and I didn't come here to lecture you. I'm just glad you're all right.'

She touched his hand in a quick gesture of apology. 'I'm sorry, too. I shouldn't be so touchy.'

He frowned. 'Actually, you have every right to be. If anyone should apologise, it's me. I thought letting you come here would make you appreciate what you had. Then I realised I was the one who lacked appreciation. I took you for granted, letting you step into your mother's shoes and putting obstacles in your way to keep you there.'

'You didn't mean any harm,' she protested.

'Good intentions are no excuse,' he said. 'I want to make it up to you.'

She stirred uncomfortably. 'There's no need, honestly.'

'Yes, there is. I wanted to tell you personally that you're the unconditional winner of our bet.'

Her eyes widened. 'But I lost. I didn't last a month by myself.'

'You would have done if it hadn't been for the storm. Dane made sure I understood that.'

Unable to sit still, she began to wander around the kitchen, picking things up and putting them down again without purpose. 'I should be glad Dane's report was favourable.'

'It wasn't a report. He wanted to be sure I didn't misunderstand the situation between you and him.' He cleared his throat noisily. 'I almost wish there was something to misunderstand. Dane Balkan is a fine man with a brilliant mind. He was on his way to becoming a real power in the finance world. I wish he would come and work for me. He could name his own price.'

The words were out before she could stop them. 'I thought he already had.'

'What? Balkan isn't working for me. There isn't enough money in the world to buy a man like him.'

She could hardly believe what she was hearing. 'You mean you didn't hire him as my watchdog?'

His laughter exploded on the air between them. 'Far from hiring him, I had to practically blackmail him into making sure no harm came to you here. Thank goodness I did, or the storm might have had tragic consequences.'

She brushed aside the last part. 'What do you mean, you blackmailed him?'

'I ran into him at the solicitor's when he was about to sign the lease for the other cottage. I gathered that he was dead keen to come here, and I planted the idea that the cottage might not be available unless he agreed to help me out.'

'How could you? I'm the only one who can deny someone access to the island.'

Her father had the grace to look ashamed. 'Luckily for both of us, Dane didn't know that.' He shifted in his seat. 'Anyway, it wasn't such an onerous task, surely? You are a lovely young woman.'

'Who reminds him of his ex-wife,' she said gloomily. 'He can't stand the sight of me.'

'And you wish you could change things?' Charlton second-guessed her.

'Am I so transparent?'

'You're forgetting how well I know you, Evelyn. Damn! When I asked him to look after you, I didn't mean you to go and fall in love with him. It seems I've hurt you again without meaning to.'

Moving up behind him, she squeezed his shoulder. 'It's all right, Dad. Some things just aren't meant to be. You did your best.'

He snorted derisively. 'I'd better stick to stocks and shares in future. I don't seem to be cut out for managing people's lives.'

She sat down opposite him at the table and refilled their coffee-cups. It was strange to hear her father admit that he had shortcomings. She wasn't sure she liked it. 'You manage thousands of lives through CCI,' she reminded him. 'You aren't doing so badly.'

His answering smile said he appreciated her comment. 'Speaking of CCI,' he said, 'you won our bet. No more hostessing duties for you, my girl. How does deputy director of the investments division sound to you?'

Her mouth dropped open. She had expected Charlton to create an opening for her in public relations or personnel, where the corporation already had women executives. But to be catapulted directly into finance was tantamount to heresy. No woman had ever held a senior position in that division. 'Oh, Dad, I don't know what to say,' she gasped.

He leaned forward. 'Then say yes. With the money you've managed for the big charities, coupled with your honours' degree, you're well qualified for the job. I'm sorry I took so long to admit it, out of pure selfishness.'

Not long ago she would have given much to hear him admit that she had a brain as well as a body. It still gratified her, but it wasn't enough. 'Thanks for the vote of confidence,' she said, sincerely, 'but I can't accept.'

He looked stunned. 'I thought it was what you wanted.'

'So did I. But staying here, I discovered I have other priorities.'

His frown deepened. 'You aren't going to turn into a drop-out, are you?'

'Maybe you see it as dropping out. I prefer to think of it as following my own star, or rather, Mum's star.'

'What does your mother have to do with this?'

She explained about finding the journal which revealed her mother's hopes for the island. 'I've decided to turn Frere into a wildlife sanctuary bearing her name,' she concluded.

Charlton made an effort to hide his disappointment. 'Whatever you want to do, you have my blessing. I've tried to run your life for long enough. I suppose I should be glad that you're your mother's daughter.'

'I'm your daughter, too,' she reminded him with an edge of pride in her voice. 'I intend to make this refuge a world authority on Tasmanian Devils. The National Parks and Wildlife Service will advise me on setting everything up properly.'

He drained his coffee-cup and stood up. 'I've no doubt it will be a success, since you want it so badly. Just don't use it as a substitute for personal happiness.' He touched her cheek. 'There are other men in the world besides Dane Balkan.'

She sighed. He was right, but it would be a long time before she would be ready to consider it. She was relieved beyond measure that Dane hadn't been in league with her father against her, but it still didn't explain why he'd taken off without a word. He must have sensed she was falling in love with him, and had gone away rather than let it go any further. She could hardly blame him. He hadn't wanted the involvement in the first place.

'I'll be all right,' she said with a touch of bravado.

If he recognised it, Charlton diplomatically ignored it. 'I know.' He dropped a light kiss on her forehead. 'I had hoped you'd come back with me, but I know better than to ask now.'

She nodded. 'How are you getting back?'

'Ned Freils is picking me up in a few minutes. He was taking a party out on D'Entrecasteaux Channel and grudgingly agreed to fit in one more passenger. But if I'm not at the jetty on time, he won't wait.'

She laughed. 'That sounds like Ned.' Even her father's wealth and power made no impact on the old sea captain.

By the time they returned to the jetty, Ned's boat was already nearing the shore. He lined the cruiser up with the jetty just long enough to allow her father to board, then opened the throttle and roared off into the bay. His party of day-trippers waved cheerfully and she waved back.

She waited until the boat was out of sight before she turned back towards the cabin. There was still the pie to put into the oven, then she intended to sit down with pen and paper and start planning the sanctuary in earnest.

At the door, she changed her mind and sat down on a bench outside. She needed a few minutes to think. So much had happened in the last hour that it was difficult to take it all in. First Dad had offered her a plum position with the corporation, then he had given his blessing when she chose to go her own way. It was more than she had any right to expect.

If only Dane had stayed, everything would have been perfect.

A crash from inside the cabin brought her to her feet. She flung open the door in time to see Henrietta feasting on her pie-filling in the middle of the kitchen floor. Bits of pastry surrounded the animal, and a cloud of flour still hung in the air. When she saw Evelyn, she let out a growl and opened her jaws wide in a threatening display.

By now, Evelyn knew that most of the threat was pure show. 'You little devil,' she said, then smiled to herself as she realised what she'd said. 'How did you get in here?'

The open window told its own story. 'Well, you'd better go out the same way,' she instructed.

Instead of making for the window, Henrietta headed for the open door which was blocked by Evelyn's legs. As the animal squeezed past her, she bent down and scooped it up. Then she noticed something unusual. Henrietta's coarse fur was matted with salt, as if she'd been exposed to sea water. And there were cobwebs caught in her ruff. Evelyn looked at them thoughtfully. 'I wonder where you've been. You look as if you've been playing in a sea cave.'

Henrietta squirmed so violently that Evelyn released her and watched the animal disappear into the undergrowth, its peculiar rocking-horse gait more pronounced because it was frightened.

It occurred to Evelyn now that she hadn't seen Henrietta since Dane had left. The Tasmanian Devil had been a special pet of his, and she had assumed that it resented Evelyn taking over. Unless...

Evelyn began to tremble with excitement at the very thought. Unless Dane was still feeding Henrietta himself.

She hadn't thought to ask her father when he had last heard from Dane, but he had only referred to the first storm, so the contact couldn't be too recent. What if Dane had never left the island?

Hiding in a cave. Her words to Henrietta came rushing back. Suddenly she knew where Dane might be. On the heels of this thought came another more sobering one. He had gone away because of her. He would be angry if she followed him to his hideout.

Still, she had to see him, even if it was for the last time. She owed him an apology for accusing him of spying on her. She also wanted to know about the sanctuary, since it was his idea.

Finding Friar's Cave posed more of a problem. She had only the vaguest idea where it was, and her ankle wasn't up to a long exploration. Then she remembered her mother's journal. There was a hand-drawn map in the back.

Sure enough, the map showed the location of both cabins and the path in between, with the waterfall and the lagoon clearly marked. Beyond the lagoon another path was shown, and she recognised it as the one she and Dane had taken when they'd set off to check on his boat.

Turning her back on the chaos in the kitchen, she pulled the door shut behind her and set off, conscious that her heart was beating faster than normal. The very idea of seeing Dane again played havoc with her senses. She would have to make an effort to control herself. He wouldn't welcome displays of affection after going to such lengths to avoid them.

For now, she had her hands full remembering the way she had to go. Her ankle was much better, but she stopped frequently to rest. She didn't want Dane to have to rescue her yet again.

It was mid-afternoon, and a heavy silence hung over the bush, disturbed only by her breathing and the faint sounds which drifted across the water from the neighbouring islands. The air was pungent with the scents of wild flowers she crushed underfoot in passing. If it hadn't been for the tree branches littering the path after the recent storms, the walk would have been idyllic.

She came to a fork and stopped. According to her mother's map, the left-hand path led down to the beach, while the right took her higher up the slope of what had been the volcano's peak in pre-history. She turned right.

Gradually the slope grew steeper and finally ended in a wall of saplings which screened the entrance to a cave. Could this be the one-armed friar's retreat from the world? She moved towards it.

In minutes, she was inside, her feet crunching on the sandy floor. After the brightness of the afternoon, it was dim and cool inside, and it took a few minutes for her eyes to adjust.

When she could see again, she found herself in a cave the size of a small room. The roof soared high overhead and was veined like the inside of a seashell. The sandy floor was criss-crossed with the distinctive footprints of the Tasmanian Devil.

Disappointment engulfed her as she took in the fact that there was no sign of Dane. Her own need of him had convinced her he would be here. A sob broke from her as she realised he had already gone. No amount of wishing and hoping could change what was.

With her hopes shattered, she turned back towards the entrance, then let out a cry of horror as a ghostly white silhouette obscured the opening. Outlined against the sky, she saw the hook which completed one arm.

Thoughts of the friar's ghost flashed through her mind. Before she could move or scream, strong arms closed around her. They were human arms, her shocked mind registered. Unbelievably, they belonged to Dane.

He supported her until she regained control of her trembling limbs. He regarded her curiously. 'You look as if you've seen a ghost.'

'I thought I had. When you appeared just now, I thought you were the one-armed friar.' Her gaze went uneasily to his arm and she saw now that he was carrying a boathook.

He looked down and made the connection. 'I was working on the boat when I heard someone up here. I brought this in case it was vandals, defacing the cave. Sorry to disappoint you if you were hoping for a ghost.'

'Believe me, I'm not disappointed.'

At once, he released her and stepped away. 'Then what are you doing here?'

'Looking for you,' she said simply.

'Well, you've found me. If it wasn't for that blasted motor, I'd have been long gone.'

So he did intend to leave. A chill settled over her and she wrapped her arms around herself. 'Can we go outside? It's cold in here.'

'As you like.' He stepped aside to let her precede him out of the cave. The sunlight dazzled her and she blinked a few times. Then she saw what she hadn't noticed on her way up here. Dane's launch was moored in the bay beneath the cave. A steep, rock-strewn path let down to the water.

He gave her his hand to help her negotiate the path, but as soon as they were safely on the beach he let her go. 'What did you want me for?'

'I came to apologise.'

He looked surprised, but quickly masked the reaction. 'There's no need. You don't owe me anything.'

'All the same, I misjudged you,' she said quietly. 'Dad came to see me this morning. He told me he hadn't hired you to spy on me. It was all he could do to get you to share the island with me. I'm sorry I didn't believe you.'

'If it makes you feel better, I accept your apology.' He sounded as if it made no difference to him either way. 'I take it your father decided not to penalise you for sharing a cabin with me?'

'Again thanks to you. He offered me an executive position with the investment division at CCI.'

Dane's face remained stony. 'So you got everything you wanted, after all. Congratulations.'

'You needn't congratulate me. I turned Dad down.'

He seemed unsurprised. 'I guess it wouldn't fit in with your plans now, would it?'

She looked at him in amazement. 'No, it won't. But how did you know?'

He drew patterns in the sand with a sneaker-clad foot. 'I overheard you talking to Jerry Cummings on the phone.'

She frowned in concentration. Had she told Jerry about the wildlife refuge? 'But I didn't tell him what I was going to do,' she said, puzzled.

His pale gaze darkened. 'Still playing games, aren't you? I heard you accept his proposal of marriage and agree to have your honeymoon here on the island.'

Her look was blank as she replayed the conversation in her head. What had she said to give him the idea she was marrying Jerry? 'He did ring to talk about marriage,' she said, slowly. 'But to someone else. When I said I accepted, it was an invitation to their wedding.'

Cracks began to appear in the stone of his expression. 'What about the honeymoon?' he asked.

'He wants to bring his bride here, since it's where he woke up to himself,' she explained. 'He thinks the island is some sort of talisman.'

There was a long silence. Dane seemed to be holding his breath. Then he expelled it in a rush. 'Maybe it is,' he said at last.

Her confusion grew. 'What are you saying?'

'I'm saying that my engine failure might just make me the luckiest man alive.'

She shook her head and curls cascaded around her face. 'I still don't understand.'

He stepped forward and gripped her shoulders in a hold so tight that she winced. Seeing it, his hold slackened but he kept her in his grasp as if he was afraid to let her go. 'Don't you know why I had to get away?' he asked, his voice hoarse.

His breath skimmed her cheek and she licked her lips nervously. 'I know you didn't want to get involved with me. I thought when we made love, you were afraid I'd use it to force you into a relationship you didn't want.'

'You're right about one thing. I didn't want to get involved with you. After my experience with Janice, I thought you were more of the same. I didn't count on falling in love with you, especially as you seemed to regard me as some sort of holiday affair.'

'I thought it was what you wanted,' she said in a low voice. 'I didn't want you thinking I was trying to trap you into anything.'

His hands travelled over her shoulders and up the slender column of her neck, to cup her face. Very gently, he pressed his lips to hers. 'Whether you meant it or not, I was caught. Fool that I was, I very nearly escaped.'

Her breathing became fast and shallow. 'Oh, Dane, I'm glad you didn't get far. I love you so much.'

It was the first time she'd admitted it aloud, and his look caressed her. 'It sounds like a very tender trap.'

'You'd better believe it.'

Miraculously, he did. 'I'll never doubt it again,' he assured her. 'I love you too much to lose you again.'

Her senses reeled as the full impact of his confession reached her. 'When did you find out?' she asked, wonder in her voice.

'I think I've known from the moment you fell at my feet at the lagoon. I fought it like hell, thinking the last thing I needed was another society type. But you were so different, I worried that I was seeing what I wanted to see in you.'

'So you set out to find fault with me,' she guessed, 'and I made it easy by the way I acted with Jerry.'

'I could have killed him for having first claim on you,' he seethed. 'Then I decided it was for the best. He was from your world. He wouldn't try to take you away from everything that makes you happy, as I wanted to do.'

'Wrong, wrong, wrong,' she muttered. 'Everything that makes me happy is right here.' She went on to tell him of her plans for the island.

As she spoke, his eyes took on a glow of enthusiasm. At the same time, he grew concerned. 'Won't you regret giving up so much?'

'Maybe,' she teased. 'In a century or so.'

With a throaty growl, he caught her in an embrace so tight that it took her breath away. 'You'd better marry me soon. A century's too long to wait.'

'I agree, although I'm already as married to you as I can be.'

'That was just a rehearsal,' he told her seriously. 'This time it will be a lifetime role.'

She lowered her lashes over misty eyes. 'You mean it gets better?'

For answer he lowered her to the hot sand and made a ferny pillow for her head. He made short work of her designer suit, and began to cover her body with fervent kisses which sent ripples of sensations over her.

Linking her arms around his neck, she drew his face down so that she could kiss him back, arching her body to meet him while the breakers foamed on to the shore close by. Overhead, the sun warmed their bodies and inflamed their passions until they could no longer remain apart. This time their togetherness bore the promise of forever.

Later, as she lay on the warm beach with Dane's body shading her, she looked up at him in wonder. 'You know, they told me you couldn't tame a Tasmanian Devil.'

His throaty growl should have warned her, but she was caught unawares when his teeth nipped the sensitive skin of her neck. 'Who are you calling tame?' he demanded, looming over her in mock threat.

She pressed her hands against his chest, feeling the throbbing vitality of him send tremors through her fingers. 'My mistake,' she said in pretend alarm.

With loving thoroughness he proceeded to show her how wrong she was, and she submitted to his lesson joyfully. A man like Dane could never be tamed. But then, neither could true love.

Harlequin Presents®

Coming Next Month

1263   A BITTER HOMECOMING Robyn Donald
Alexa returns home to find that Leon Venetos believes all the scandal broadcast about her And he wastes no time showing his contempt in unfair treatment of her Yet Alexa can't fight the attraction that binds them together

1264   WILD PASSAGE Vanessa Grant
Neil Turner, looking for crew for his boat, signs on Serena. He has no idea that although she's lived with sailing for years, it's only been in her dreams. He soon finds out as they start down the west coast of the United States that her practical experience is actually nil!

1265   EQUAL OPPORTUNITIES Penny Jordan
Sheer desperation leads Kate Oakley to employ a man as nanny for nine-month-old Michael, her friend's orphaned baby And while Rick Evans comes with impeccable references, he has his own motives for wanting to be in her life.

1266   WITH NO RESERVATIONS Leigh Michaels
Faced with running the old family hotel, Lacey Clinton soon realizes she isn't properly qualified to restore it. Selling to rival hotelier Damon Kendrick seems the answer—until she learns he doesn't want the hotel unless Lacey comes with it.

1267   DREAMS ON FIRE Kathleen O'Brien
Megan Farrell already dreads locking horns with the new owner of the New Orleans rare book shop where she works. But even she has no idea how easily this man can destroy her firm ideas about the past—and especially those about love and passion.

1268   DANCE TO MY TUNE Lilian Peake
Jan accepts as just another job the assignment of tracking down Rik Steele and reconciling him and his father. When she falls in love with her quarry, she has a hard time convincing him that she's not just interested in the money.

1269   LEAP IN THE DARK Kate Walker
When a stranger kidnaps Ginny and the two children she's temporarily looking after, Ginny doesn't know where to turn for comfort. All her instincts tell her to turn to Ross Hamilton—but he's the man holding them captive.

1270   DO YOU REMEMBER BABYLON Anne Weale
Singer Adam Rocquaine, idolized the world over, can have any woman he wants. And it seems he wants Maggie. She knows a brief fling in the public eye would leave her miserable—yet she wonders if she has the strength to say no.

Available in May wherever paperback books are sold, or through Harlequin Reader Service:

In the U.S.
901 Fuhrmann Blvd.
P.O. Box 1397
Buffalo, N.Y. 14240-1397

In Canada
P.O. Box 603
Fort Erie, Ontario
L2A 5X3

**In April, Harlequin brings you the
world's most popular romance author**

JANET
DAILEY

No Quarter Asked

Out of print since 1974!

After the tragic death of her father, Stacy's world is shattered. She needs to get away by herself to sort things out. She leaves behind her boyfriend, Carter Price, who wants to marry her. However, as soon as she arrives at her rented cabin in Texas, Cord Harris, owner of a large ranch, seems determined to get her to leave. When Stacy has a fall and is injured, Cord reluctantly takes her to his own ranch. Unknown to Stacy, Carter's father has written to Cord and asked him to keep an eye on Stacy and try to convince her to return home. After a few weeks there, in spite of Cord's hateful treatment that involves her working as a ranch hand and the return of Lydia, his ex-fiancée, by the time Carter comes to escort her back, Stacy knows that she is in love with Cord and doesn't want to go.

**Watch for *Fiesta San Antonio* in July and
For Bitter or Worse in September.**

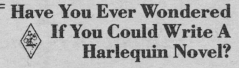

Have You Ever Wondered If You Could Write A Harlequin Novel?

Here's great news—Harlequin is offering a series of cassette tapes to help you do just that. Written by Harlequin editors, these tapes give practical advice on how to make your characters—and your story—come alive. There's a tape for each contemporary romance series Harlequin publishes.

Mail order only

All sales final

TO: *Harlequin Reader Service*
      Audiocassette Tape Offer
      P.O. Box 1396
      Buffalo, NY   14269-1396

I enclose a check/money order payable to HARLEQUIN READER SERVICE® for $9.70 ($8.95 plus 75¢ postage and handling) for EACH tape ordered for the total sum of $_____*
Please send:

[ ] Romance and Presents   [ ] Intrigue
[ ] American Romance   [ ] Temptation
[ ] Superromance   [ ] All five tapes ($38.80 total)

Signature_____
                                    (please print clearly)
Name:_____
Address:_____
State:_____ Zip:_____

*Iowa and New York residents add appropriate sales tax.   AUDIO-H

H A R L E Q U I N
American Romance®

Live the

Rocky Mountain Magic

Become a part of the magical events at The Stanley Hotel in the Colorado Rockies, and be sure to catch its final act in April 1990 with #337 RETURN TO SUMMER by Emma Merritt.

Three women friends touched by magic find love in a very special way, the way of enchantment. Hayley Austin was gifted with a magic apple that gave her three wishes in BEST WISHES (#329). Nicki Chandler was visited by psychic visions in SIGHT UNSEEN (#333). Now travel into the past with Kate Douglas as she meets her soul mate in RETURN TO SUMMER #337.

ROCKY MOUNTAIN MAGIC—All it takes is an open heart.

If you missed any of Harlequin American Romance Rocky Mountain Magic titles, and would like to order it, send your name, address, and zip or postal code, along with a check or money order for $2.50 plus 75¢ postage and handling, payble to Harlequin Reader Service to:

In the U.S.
901 Fuhrmann Blvd.
Box 1325
Buffalo, NY 14269

In Canada
P.O. Box 609
Fort Erie, Ontario
L2A 5X3

Please specify book title with your order.

RMM3-1